WINTER OF DISCONTENT

SHAPE UP OR SHIFT OUT BOOK 2

MANDY ROSKO

WINTER OF DISCONTENT

SHAPE UP OR SHIFT OUT BOOK 2

Roquette Avery, a white raccoon shifter, is terrified that someone will recognize her for who she truly is: a thief who's just recently turned her life around and is yearning to find her fated mate.

Harmony Baer doesn't seem to care about Roquette's past, though. She's personally invited Roquette to the annual Christmas party she hosts with her sisters. Roquette is nervous but excited until a nefarious-looking vampire shows up to crash the party and tells Roquette she looks *exactly* like another raccoon shifter she's met—a raccoon shifter who stole something very valuable from the vampire's home.

Before the vampire can harm Roquette, her bodyguard intervenes. He shines a glowing red eye on Roquette and grabs her with his metallic arm, insisting she flee the party. Too bad. This raccoon is not about to jet. No one gets to tell her what to do, no matter *who* she might resemble.

And besides, Mr. bodyguard is pretty sexy, and Roquette's got a sneaking suspicion that *he's* her fated mate.

Roquette Avery's attendance at a Christmas party thrown by *the* Baer sisters was comparable to letting a muddy dog climb up onto the table and give a good shake all over the festive ham.

The three Baers—Sheri, Harmony, and Esme—were well-known in the shifter community. Not only were they bear shifters, but they were also very powerful witches, and rumored to be some kind of ancient beings, though they looked like middle-aged human women.

Esme was the most sought-after Baer. She was a matchmaker with an impeccable record. She was also nearly impossible to track down. So when Roquette had stopped into the Baer's shop, she wasn't surprised when she was told that Esme wasn't in.

But she *was* surprised when Esme's sister, Harmony, stopped to chat with her... and ended up inviting her to the sister's elusive Christmas party.

Now Roquette stood outside the party, watching others step inside while trying to figure out what she was doing there. She gripped the gift for the hostess in her hand—a bottle of champagne that was way too damned cheap for a place like this.

"Just show up, you can meet my sister there," Harmony had told Roquette. "Be yourself. You only need to come on over, drink, and have fun."

Yeah.

No.

It didn't matter what the woman said or how casual she promised the event would be. The lavish mansion the Baer sisters had rented for the event was enough to warn Roquette away, but the guests walking in confirmed her suspicions.

Roquette had a sense about people. She could tell who came from money and influence. It was in the way they carried themselves. In the confidence they exuded while joining the party, seamlessly blending into the warmth and lights, and sounds of laughter.

Not to mention their nice clothing, shoes, and accessories. That was another thing Roquette was good at picking out. She could tell who wore the five hundred dollar boots and jackets, whose jewelry was the real deal and not just made out of glass.

And the people walking past her definitely had the authentic stuff.

Roquette definitely didn't belong here. Not with her self-trimmed long blond hair, cheap leggings, and decade-old black sequined sweater.

She should go home. It wasn't like she and Harmony were friends. They hardly knew each other. Roquette didn't have any personal connection to Harmony, Esme, or Sheri Baer...

Definitely made no sense. Roquette was totally leaving.

Except her stupid feet refused to move, and now it looked like she was stuck.

"Are you coming inside?"

Roquette blinked. Standing like she was on the walkway leading to the party, it only made sense that someone would eventually stop and wonder what her problem was.

"Yeah, eventually. I was just... gathering my thoughts," Roquette mumbled.

More people walked by, paying her no attention, but of the couple who stopped—a tall man with black hair and a plaid scarf and a woman whose blond hair was held back with feather ear muffs that were whiter than the snow around them—it was the woman who smiled and kept talking to her.

"You don't have to be nervous. If you're here, then the Baers invited you, right?"

"Right," Roquette nodded, but only because it didn't sound like the woman was prying or trying to weed out the riff-raff. It really sounded like she was trying to make polite conversation.

"Then you don't have anything to worry about. Are you here with someone, or are you going to ask for Esme's help with that?"

"Uh..." Jesus, that was direct for a lady who didn't know Roquette's first name.

"She paired the two of us together. Either way, don't worry about it. She's the nicest lady you'll ever meet. Might ask you to do some... odd things to get yourself paired, but it's always worth it."

"Like... she doesn't ask for money?"

The couple looked at each other. The man shrugged and said nothing. Roquette figured he was the shy type.

"Not for us, anyway," said the woman. "I'm not sure if she's asked for money from anyone else. I don't think so. Anyway, enough of that. Come on inside with us."

"No, no, I'm good. I really was just thinking about what I was going to say." Roquette lifted her small box with the cheap wine bottle inside. "I assume everyone won't mind the extra booze?"

The blonde laughed. Her partner looked as though he was getting cold.

"All right, but come and find me if you're feeling shy. I promise, I used to be just like you. You don't have anything to worry about."

With that, the couple turned and went through the front doors with everyone else.

They were... a lovely couple. They looked like they walked right out of a Hallmark Christmas movie.

Roquette kind of wished they'd been bitchy, instead of so nice and eager to help, suggesting the whole party might be full of folks like them.

So what was Roquette's problem?

The sounds of laughter, music, and general chatter became louder every time the door opened, only to die down when it shut again.

As though telling Roquette she was missing her chance to enter that magical portal where everything was all right, everyone got along, and no one cared about anyone's shady past or how much—or how little—they had in their pockets.

Maybe she would hang outside for a bit longer. Maybe explore the house a little, from the outside.

That sounded like a plan. At least like enough of a plan to kill some more time while she worked up her courage to go inside.

Roquette walked away from the front door, but not because she was a coward who was leaving. She was just going to take her time before going inside.

The mansion the Baer sisters rented for the party was beautiful. They went all out on the festivities, that was for sure.

The place looked like the sort of Winter Wonderland that Roquette would have dreamed about living in when she was growing up in a shitty neighborhood on the bad side of town.

No decorations like this on her childhood home or that of her neighbors. There hadn't been much money for Christmas decorations. Not for Halloween, either.

Roquette's Halloweens were usually spent going out to one of the richer neighborhoods in old sheets to look like ghosts, then hitting the same houses again in dollar store masks. The candies and sodas provided padded her school lunches for months, though her parents usually went through the sodas in a couple of days.

Christmases were a little different. Her parents did try for that holiday. Despite all their flaws, and the many, many things they could have done better, they did try to make Christmases half-decent.

They always had a tree—one her father would chop down for free from God-only-knew-where—and decorated with more dollar store or thrift store ornaments. Roquette always thought the ornaments were all very pretty, and it never mattered to her that nothing matched, either.

Her presents had been small, cheaply bought, but well-loved. Coloring books and pencils, little nail polishes, and candies. Anything that could come from a dollar store, but her mom always made sure to buy her one brand new Barbie doll every year. It didn't matter which one it was. That had been Roquette's big gift of the year.

Roquette loved Christmas.

Maybe this party, all lit up the way it was, reminded her of that. The sisters clearly had a theme going, but there was also a certain... festiveness to it that reminded Roquette of her mom and dad.

Roquette walked around the house. If anyone looked at her, she would have the excuse that she was just admiring the blinking lights and various decorations. At least she wasn't the only one. There were plenty of others meandering around, admiring the lights, the Santas, the blow-up reindeer, and the many gingerbread houses and gingerbread people.

There was hardly an inch of the place that hadn't been touched up.

With the sky getting darker sooner in the day, the bright lights were more than enough to help set Roquette at ease. The sounds of laughter, music and general talking that floated to her from inside the mansion itself warmed her.

As though she was welcomed there. As though she belonged and wasn't just some random nobody raccoon shifter, but was an old friend of the Baers.

Right. She was going inside. The cold had started to seep through Roquette's jacket, hat, and gloves, and the time had come to face the music. To say hello to Harmony and see what she might have in mind for a misfit like Roquette.

CHAPTER

TWO

As she walked toward the entry, a new couple stepped out in front of her, blocking her path. They seemed to appear out of nowhere, which was odd because the woman stuck out like a sore thumb—someone Roquette would have seen from a mile away, not just when she stepped right in front of her.

Her distinctiveness wasn't just from her heavy red coat. It was the seasonal color that many others also wore. No, what made her stand out the most to Roquette was her height—increased by the heels she wore.

In the snow. Heels. Not the chunky heels normal to winter boots, either. Stilettos, like the ones the red-coat woman wore, could be used as a weapon to stab someone through the heart if needed.

Usually, Roquette would have stepped around them, side-eyeing the Stilettos before going on about her business.

But something compelled her to stop. She felt she *needed* to say hello to them.

Was it a pay-it-forward type of thing? Maybe because

the other couple had been so nice to her, she felt a need to welcome the new people?

"Hey there," Roquette called toward them.

The woman ignored her, or maybe didn't hear her. She kept looking up at the house itself... but the man with her?

He turned his head the slightest bit to look at who dared speak to them.

His eyes remained hidden underneath sunglasses, but Roquette didn't need to see his whole face to know he was an extremely handsome man. Tall—very tall—with thick black hair, exquisite bone structure, and thick lips pursed in annoyance. His jaw, covered in a short black beard, remained fixed tight to tell Roquette that her company was not desired, and she thought she might have seen him push his straight nose a bit higher in the air after assessing her.

Wow. Despite his unfriendly demeanor, Roquette couldn't help but feel drawn to him.

Probably something ridiculously attractive people just have to deal with from us common folk, she thought.

Roquette expected the woman to place a possessive arm on him or something, but she didn't. In fact, Roquette noticed that the man stood a few steps behind her. Not beside her, like he was her lover or spouse, but just behind her.

Maybe he was her secretary? An assistant of some kind?

Roquette stepped to the side and came around the couple's side, assessing the woman's face.

Steely, unamused, and cold.

Roquette didn't think the weather had anything to do with it.

Still, she tried again to offer words of encouragement. "Are you both coming inside? I was just about to go in."

That feeling of not belonging there, or not being one of those people, came back with a vengeance.

No. She might not be rich and beautiful like the others, but that didn't mean she had to go anywhere. Harmony had invited her. Roquette was *supposed* to be there.

"Harmony invited me to the party," Roquette fumbled with her words clumsily. "Have you seen her around? I was just going to look for her."

"I care nothing for that woman." The marble lady finally spoke, sparing Roquette a glance, her green eyes flashing.

The tiny hairs on the back of Roquette's neck stood up, and her instincts screamed for her to run as a realization came to her...

Vampire.

The word ghosted into her head without her realizing it, like it had snuck in there to drink her blood when she slept.

No. That was stupid. She shouldn't feel afraid like that. Vampires weren't dangerous just because they were vampires. Roquette didn't want to let herself think such terrible things, so she pushed it right out of her head and smiled as though the woman in front of her wasn't being a bitch.

"So, not friends then. Were you still planning on coming inside?"

Did this lady not get an invite? Was she there to crash the party?

The man shook his head ever so slightly, in a way that reminded Roquette of how people regarded her when they caught her dumpster diving.

Which she was definitely not doing right then.

"Is there a problem?" Roquette asked.

The man straightened his shades on the bridge of his perfect nose and turned his head away from her, not bothering with an answer.

The whole situation was getting a little too weird.

"Are you both okay?" More and more, she felt something wasn't right with them. "Yeah. So, anyway... It's cold out here, and I'm going to go inside. You can both walk in with me if you want."

"Why would we wish to do that?" The woman wasn't just cold. She was a complete bitch. This was why Roquette hated talking to strangers.

"I was just trying to be nice, but never mind," Roquette said, stepping past them and toward the steps leading up to the door. "I can see you're good. Sorry to have bothered you with my attempt at friendliness."

"You look like her," the woman said.

"What?" Roquette stopped and looked back at the pair. The woman was suddenly staring at her like she wanted to step in for a closer look...

Like Roquette might be someone she absolutely despised.

O-kaaaaaaaay.

Best to keep moving. Roquette hurried up the front stairs, only turning back to look at the couple one last time when she reached the door.

She couldn't stop herself. She just wanted to make sure they weren't stalking behind her.

They weren't. In fact, the woman had vanished, though how she could have walked away so quickly in those stilettos was a mystery.

The man, on the other hand, the one with the mysterious sunglasses, the strong jaw, and wide-set shoulders... he was still there. He looked back at her, and Roquette saw his chest suddenly rise, as though he was just as shocked as she was that she'd looked back.

She didn't dwell on it. Not the oddball situation or the twisting in her stomach when she and that man looked at each other.

Roquette moved her ass toward the front of the house and got herself inside before anything else could happen.

THREE

Roquette breathed a heavy sigh of overly warm, indoor air when she finally left the strange couple behind.

Her heart wouldn't stop hammering, and the sudden change from cold to hot wasn't helping anything either.

That had genuinely spooked her. She hadn't felt like that since the first time she'd been caught sniffing around in the neighbor's trash bin, but in her defense, they were throwing out some amazing stuff. Barely worn clothes, some old dolls that were still good, and even books.

And who threw out books?

The way Roquette had seen it, she'd been saving the stuff, but Mr. Slatt had run out of his house screaming bloody murder. It had been enough to make Roquette more careful about when she went sniffing around in the bins.

This felt like that, only... a little off-kilter. The racing of her heart was there, but also something... exhilarating.

Should she tell someone about the strange couple? It was too odd. That woman clearly didn't have an invite if she was skulking around outside.

Maybe she and the Baers were enemies?

Except, Roquette didn't want to be that kind of person since she was all too familiar with being the target of such disdain.

"Does she have an invite?"

"Who asked her to come?"

"Are you lost?"

Did Roquette really want to be like them?

"Can I take your coat?"

Roquette jumped as a woman who looked like she could be a living, breathing Barbie doll spoke.

"I'm so sorry!" the woman laughed softly as Roquette placed a hand over her heart to calm herself. "Did I startle you?"

"N-no, not at all." Roquette immediately shrugged off her jacket, handing it over to the woman. "Sorry, I was just kind of lost in thought. The house is beautiful," Roquette added quickly to cover for her strange reaction.

"I know, right?" The woman placed Roquette's jacket gently over her arm like she was caring for an expensive piece of clothing and not some many seasons old, off-the-rack knock-off. "The sisters go all out. How do you know them?"

Roquette didn't mind that the woman was fishing for information. She figured most of the people in the enormous party had to be friends or clients. That is, clients of Esme, the matchmaker sister, from the look of all the happy couples.

"Just a lucky person given an invite. What about you?"

The woman raised her hand, proudly showing off her engagement ring. "But not because of Esme. I might be one of two people here she didn't set up, but she's met Mark, and as long as she approves, I think it means I picked well."

"That checks out," Roquette said. She realized the

woman probably had better things to do than chat with her all night, and besides, Roquette had to remember why she was there in the first place. "Uh, is Harmony around here? She told me to find her when I arrived."

"You'll find her next to the tree."

Roquette glanced off to the side. Through the sea of people, she could make out multiple trees.

"No, sorry, the *big* tree," Barbie said. "In the sitting room. Down the hall at the very end. Gingerbread men everywhere. You can't miss it."

"Great, thanks," Roquette said, watching Barbie neatly tuck her jacket into a closet. It seemed greeting folks was her job for the night because she didn't go anywhere else. She just remained standing there, waiting for anyone else to walk by in need of lightning up.

"Can I grab your name?" Roquette felt terrible for thinking of her as *Barbie*.

"Emily, and I'll be here most of the night, but if you want to leave and I'm not around, you can grab your jacket. This is just a formality. Everyone here trusts each other not to go through anyone's pockets."

"Okay, thanks." Roquette laughed nervously, that phrasing hitting a little too close to home.

Little did her new friend know that Roquette was exactly the sort of person most people wanted to guard their pockets against.

She walked away before Emily could get a feel for what type of person Roquette actually was, and set off to find Harmony.

There really was a small sea of people there. Roquette couldn't believe that just a few years ago, cops would've been outside in hazmat suits to break up the party, citing possible contamination or super spreader threats.

Luckily, there were no longer any issues with strange diseases making their way through the world. It seemed like since then, people were making up for lost time by packing themselves into any and all events they could get to.

Like sardines in a can. Or kids at a rave.

The party wasn't quite a rave. It was too bright, and the music wasn't exactly enough to induce head-banging, but Roquette was forced to squeeze through more than one set of tightly packed bodies.

The Baers knew lots of people, it seemed.

"There you are!"

Someone from behind grabbed her by the wrist, yanking her back and around. Roquette's immediate instinct was to fight, but that was nearly impossible because of the hand on her wrist and all the bodies surrounding her.

Thankfully, because otherwise, it would have been really horrible for Roquette to have raised her fist toward Harmony Baer herself.

Harmony, all smiles, her orange curls bouncing around her head like a halo, pulled Roquette in for a tight hug. "I am so happy you made it!"

"You are?" Roquette asked, stunned that the woman made it sound like she and Roquette were old friends and not like Roquette was just a nuisance who wanted to ask for a favor.

"Of course!" Harmony looked over her outfit and smiled widely. "You look so pretty!"

"Thank you," Roquette mumbled, unable to believe someone so fashionable would offer a little old unstylish raccoon such a compliment. Especially someone in high-waisted black pants, a silver sequined cutout shirt, and the most unbelievably shiny silver shoes that Roquette had ever seen. "You, though... wow, you look fabulous."

Harmony laughed. "Thank you. This is just one of my outfits for tonight. That's not a brag. You see, my sister Esme has so many friends in the fashion industry that send us clothes and I'm never able to wear them all, so I use events like these as a chance to finally show some off."

"Oh." Roquette didn't know how to respond to that. She *wished* she could be so lucky to have more clothes than she could ever wear in one lifetime.

"Come with me. We'll get something to drink." Harmony looped their arms together, and again, Roquette couldn't get over the fact that Harmony was treating her like they were good friends.

CHAPTER

FOUR

IT WARMED HER UP FROM THE INSIDE OUT. ROQUETTE HADN'T realized a stranger could make her feel comfortable and welcomed, but somehow, Harmony did.

Harmony led her through the ocean of people, passed the many gingerbread men and blinking reindeer, to a long table loaded with glistening pastries, sparkling crystal punch bowls, and porcelain statues.

Well, what Roquette at first *thought* were porcelain statues until someone cut into one, and she realized they were cakes in the shapes of more gingerbread men, more Santas, and even an elf. They were probably made by Sheri, the Baer sister known to love to bake.

Roquette sure as hell wouldn't have wanted to be the first to cut into one of those beauties.

"Alcohol or non-alcohol?" Harmony asked, grabbing a clean champagne flute from the pyramid on the table.

"Uh, non, please." Roquette didn't want to get tipsy and offend anyone. This seemed like the sort of high society place where one wrong move could mean she would be banished forever.

And never have another chance to ask for Harmony's help.

Harmony looked at her, still smiling but with her eyes slightly narrowed.

As though she knew what was going on through Roquette's mind.

Finally, Harmony shrugged, pulling a ladle from the crystal punch bowl with the non-alcoholic sign in front of it.

Harmony served herself from the alcohol one.

"Drink up," Harmony handed Roquette the flute, then placed her arm around Roquette's shoulders, leaning in. "Don't be nervous, sweetheart. We're all family here, and I doubt you'll be the first to make a fool of yourself at a party."

"That's not... well, not the *only* thing I'm worried about." She could have kicked herself the instant the words left her mouth.

Harmony didn't miss a beat. "I know, and don't worry about that either. I'll understand if a few little things get misplaced. Happens all the time at large gatherings."

Harmony drank from her glass while Roquette felt the cold hand of terror grip her heart.

Did Harmony know? She couldn't know. There was no way....

But this was the woman whose sister was said to be able to find people's perfect matches. Their fated mates.

If Esme could do something like that, then it was entirely possible that Harmony would figure out which raccoon shifter might have somewhat sticky fingers.

Most people who found out about that little personality flaw didn't act so casual about it. And they weren't even in the Baer sisters' house. They were at a place rented for the party. Meaning they were liable for anything damaged or stolen.

And Harmony didn't care?

"Are you... sure you understand...?"

"I've told Esme all about you, but we'll talk business later," Harmony said, lowering her glass from her lips, her eyes dancing. "You should go and have some fun."

"Oh, but I was really hoping we could—"

"Joanne!" Harmony called, cutting Roquette off and waving her hand in the air at someone across the room. "There you are! I was hoping you would make it."

Harmony was gone in a flutter. She somehow managed to navigate her way through the crowded party like she was made of water, off to give another woman a hug through the mass of people.

Roquette tried not to feel disappointed. Just because she was going to have to wait a bit longer didn't mean anything.

The sight of all those glistening sweets and cakes, some of which sparkled better than any gemstone, was enough to make her feel a little better.

Right. This was a party. Of course Esme didn't want to get right to business.

Roquette could be patient and wait, especially when there was chocolate cake to be had.

She picked up one of the small plates and placed a few treats on it. A slice of chocolate cake from the cut-up elf cake, a few chocolate-dipped strawberries, a chocolate drizzled cream puff, and a gingerbread man cookie for good measure.

The first taste brightened her right up.

Chocolate fixed *everything*.

And helped her mingle. She spoke to different guests,

with the topic of conversation usually being how everyone knew the Baers. Many seemed to figure out quickly that Roquette was a hopeful client for Esme—likely because she seemed to be there without a date—and they assured her that the best was yet to come.

That *Esme had her ways.*

And to *trust the process.*

The best part was that the longer she stayed, the less Roquette worried.

Worried that her secret would come out or that she would face any temptations.

No one knew who she was. Roquette could just be... normal.

As normal as someone could be when they were a shifter.

But most of the others at the party were also shifters... so Roquette felt like she fit in more than she had anywhere else before.

Eventually, with the heat of the house from all those shifter bodies pressed together, Roquette needed to take a break and go outside.

She wasn't the only one with that idea. The outside was full of people with cups of hot cocoa, walking around the ice sculpture displays.

The garden lamps shone down on the snow and cast a lovely glow on the backdrop of a starry sky. Roquette hadn't bothered grabbing her coat, but there was no need. She only intended to stay outside for a few minutes of fresh air.

"After today," she said to herself. "Everything will be different. In a good way."

"It will be if you get the hell out of here. Right now."

A hand gripped Roquette's shoulder tightly and whirled her around.

The aggressive move triggered something in her brain. She flashed back to a time when a homeowner had caught her pilfering his expensive watch collection and attacked.

Now, she automatically defended herself with a swinging fist.

And she damn near broke her hand on her assailant's solid jaw.

His head snapped to the side, his sunglasses flying off, but he looked more shocked than hurt.

It was that guy from before. The man who had been standing with the rude lady in red.

"Oh my God, I'm so sorry!" Finally remembering exactly where she was, Roquette realized she'd just punched a possible guest. She sought out his sunglasses in the snow—why was anyone wearing sunglasses at night?—fished them out and handed them to him.

"I'm so sorry. I didn't realize...." She suddenly saw why

someone would wear sunglasses at night when she caught a look at his eyes.

One of which glowed a bright shade of red.

Roquette paused, taken aback by the sight of it. At first, she thought it might've had something to do with whatever his shifter form was. Many shifters had eyes that turned red when they were angry, and she had just punched him, so it would make sense...

But only one eye glowed red, while the other stayed a bright shade of green. Plus, the pupil of the red eye dilated and contracted quickly, over and over again.

Reminding Roquette of a camera lens or something in a machine.

"Uh, here." She handed him back the sunglasses.

He snatched them, pressing them back over his eyes, hiding what was there.

"I'm sorry. I didn't mean—"

"Never mind that. You need to get out of here."

Her heart paused. That was what he'd said right before grabbing her, but she hadn't processed the words until now. "Why? I was invited."

She'd been made. That had to be it. Someone knew what she used to do for a living, and they wanted her gone before she could snatch the good silverware.

Except that wasn't the explanation she received.

"She doesn't appreciate being seen. You wouldn't leave before, and you look..." He stopped, taking a breath as though calming himself. "Are you related to a woman named Rita Procyon?"

"What? No, I don't think so. I've never heard that name before," she answered. Well, she hadn't heard the *full* name before, but she was pretty sure that Procyon meant raccoon...

"Pay attention!" Mr. Sunglasses snapped his fingers in front of her face.

"Sorry! Sorry."

"And stop apologizing. You don't need to focus on anything other than getting out of here."

"But why? Because I look like someone else? Someone named Rita Procyon?"

"Yes, exactly that." Mr. Sunglasses grabbed her arm, his black leather gloves not cushioning the cold and steely feel of his fingers underneath.

"Ow, hey!" Roquette pushed back against him, but it was like shoving against a vice and a brick wall.

Strong, as many shifters were, but this was different.

Roquette had been grabbed before by humans and shifters alike. Regular folk, police officers, and bad guys of all kinds, but none of them had fingers that dug into her like that before.

Mr. Sunglasses came in closer, towering over her, his words spoken through clenched teeth. "You *need* to leave."

A sliver of fear worked through her, and then anger.

With a new strength, Roquette pushed against his chest, yanking her arm back hard, though his fingers didn't seem to want to let go. She swore they felt like they were made of metal, and it hurt like hell to escape his grasp.

"I don't have to go anywhere! I was invited! By Harmony!" she shouted, rubbing the sore spot on her arm.

"I don't care. This has nothing to do..." he stopped himself.

"It does have to do with Harmony, doesn't it?"

"Not her specifically, but that's not the point. You cannot stay here."

The wheels in Roquette's head started to turn, slowly at

first, and then faster and faster as her imagination concocted terrible scenarios.

What if something was about to go down?

Something well outside of her pay grade.

"All right. I'll go."

A dark brow rose up above the sunglasses to tell Roquette that he definitely didn't believe her.

"I will," she insisted. "I'll leave. I just need to grab my coat."

"Leave without it."

"Are you kidding me? I'm only wearing a sweater! I'll grab my jacket and leave."

And while I'm inside, I'll make sure to find Harmony and tell her that there are a couple of weirdos outside who seemed to be planning some trouble...

She turned quickly as though that was the end of the conversation, but she should have known better. Turning her back on an enemy was always a bad idea.

Of course he grabbed her again. Of *course* he was ready for her this time when she tried punching him.

She should have expected the arm that trapped her and the hand that clamped tightly over her mouth while Mr. Sunglasses carried her off.

Why wasn't anyone helping her? Could they not see Roquette struggling against the man who was carting her off?

"It's going to be fine. I'm getting you out of here," he said, grunting when she elbowed him in the stomach.

Finally, something that didn't feel like it was made of metal. She slammed her elbow into his stomach again and again as he made it farther and farther away from the lights of the house and the garden lamps.

Not that it mattered. She had excellent night vision. Raccoons, after all, were nocturnal.

Wait, duh! What are you doing?

The moment Roquette remembered she could become a small furry mammal, she shifted faster than she'd ever changed in her entire life. The fear of getting dragged off and raped in the snowy woods was a hell of a motivator.

She didn't bother taking the time to make sure her clothes would survive. All of her thoughts and efforts were focused on escaping her captor.

And as she'd hoped, the sudden change in her shape and size had the intended effect.

Mr. Sunglasses fumbled with his hold on her as she shrank. His hands felt around in the bundle of fur and clothes, trying to figure out what he could grab hold of.

Too late, jerk!

She dropped from his arms, a fat little trash panda plopping to the ground.

Success!

She made to scuttle off to safety, but her clothes—*her fucking oversized sweater that she loved so much*—acted as a net around her body. In her sudden panic, she couldn't find an exit. *Where was the damn neck hole?*

That gave Mr. Sunglasses plenty of time to pin her in the trap of her own making. He scooped her up in her sweater, using it as a makeshift bag.

She wasn't done yet, though. Roquette bit down on the first thing that came close to her little teeth and...

Fucking ouch!

She yanked her mouth back when it felt like she'd bitten down on a steel metal bar, screeching and squealing, fighting against the sweater snare. Her raccoon sounds were wilder than she'd ever made in her entire life.

"Stop it," Mr. Sunglasses snapped. "Calm down. *Calm down.* I'm not going to hurt you."

Yeah, right.

Roquette flinched slightly when she felt the man's hands stroking her through the sweater.

Petting her. Like he was trying to calm her down.

"I won't hurt you. I promise."

CHAPTER

SIX

HER OPTIMISTIC SIDE WANTED TO BELIEVE HIM, BUT SHE JUST couldn't let it go that he was dragging her away from the party against her will. She hissed her displeasure.

"You don't know what's going on," he continued. "And that's fair. I can't tell you everything, but you *do* look a lot like Rita—someone Lilly hates. On top of that, you've seen Lilly's face, long enough that you could describe it, and we weren't supposed to be here."

I knew it! They were party crashers, and she'd nailed them.

Despite that knowledge, she began to relax in response to his calming tone and soothing touch.

"I'm just going to get you out of there."

He moved the sweater around, and when the neck hole appeared, Roquette moved for it.

"Easy. Easy now," he said, grabbing her again and stopping her before she could dart to freedom.

Exposed in all of her raccoon glory, she hissed and snapped at him.

He simply stared at her in response. His sunglasses had

come off again—she must have knocked them from his face in the tussle—and both his eyes blinked at her.

It was that same confused gawking she received anytime someone saw her for the first time and tried to piece together what sort of animal she was.

A woman who turned into a raccoon was one thing, but people expected a raccoon to have a black mask, grey fur, and a poofy ringed tail.

She had the tiny, agile hands and the beady eyes that the other raccoons had, but her mask was more of a dark brown, and the rest was fully white.

"What... are you?"

Roquette growled, and he actually let her go, staring down at her as though trying to determine what species of oversized rat she was.

She hated that look.

And yet, she couldn't run away from him either. It was like her body was frozen, but it had nothing to do with the cold.

Looking up at him that way, the two of them locked in a strange, tentative peace, she couldn't help but realize that his eyes were Christmas-colored. Red and green... even if one eye looked like it belonged to *The Terminator*.

She processed what she was looking at. His body had been modified. The eye was some sort of biomechatronic thing.

How much of the rest of him had been enhanced that way?

She remembered his steely grip...

Roquette snapped herself out of it.

What the hell was she doing? This guy had just tried to kidnap her, and now they were both standing there, staring at each other as though waiting for the other to grow a second head.

Still, the man was handsome. Handsome enough that Roquette decided to forgive herself for getting distracted, but she wasn't about to risk her life over it.

She shifted back into her human form, and she swore she saw a dusting of color in Mr. Sunglasses cheeks before he turned away from her naked body.

She shook the leaves from her sweater, dressing quickly, and was shocked when he held out her ankle boots and pants.

"Here," he said after shaking out her pants. "I think you should find your underwear yourself."

Was he embarrassed? That was... really cute.

"I don't wear any."

"Of course you don't." He kept his face turned away from her while he replaced his sunglasses.

Well, well, well. Wasn't that adorable...

Roquette stuck one foot into her pants. "So, you were going to kidnap me, but you're getting all shy about whether or not I wear panties?"

The other foot went next, and then a sock she found. A fresh shift left her body heated, but that would only last another couple of minutes before she wouldn't be able to take it anymore. She needed to get some layers on her.

"I was *not* kidnapping you."

"Uh-huh. Because covering my mouth and dragging me off into the woods is definitely not weird. Or creepy."

He finally looked at her again, a glare on his face, the red in his mechanical eye seeming to glow that much brighter.

"I am not a pervert or a rapist. So get that thought out of your head."

He sounded so insulted and so angry about it that for a moment, she felt guilty for accusing him.

But then she reminded herself that she didn't know this guy, or the woman he claimed to be protecting her from, so screw him! He'd grabbed Roquette and hauled her off against her will, and that meant she had nothing to feel bad about.

"Don't go dragging women off against their will, and maybe you won't be charged with attempted atrocities."

"Whatever. You're dressed now, and I need to get you out of here before she notices I'm gone."

He reached for her, grabbing her arm again.

"You are hurting me." Roquette had to clench her teeth against the pain that his tight squeeze gave her.

He seemed shocked. He loosened his grip, but he didn't let her go. She knew it would be difficult for her to break free this time, now that he knew she was willing to shift and fight it out with him.

"That better?" he asked, as though he cared.

"Barely," Roquette snapped. "Why do I have to leave again? Because your boss is a bitch who doesn't like that I remind her of someone? Who cares?"

"*You* will care if Lilly thinks you can give her information."

"Uh, why would she think that? I don't know the person she thinks I look like."

He narrowed his eyes. "Your shifter animal... is a raccoon?"

Roquette rolled her eyes. "Why can't anyone ever tell right away? Yes, I am. I just don't have the coloring. You know not all raccoons have those striped tails and grey fur, right?"

"Jesus Christ," the man muttered before letting let off a

slew of other curse words that even a thief like her was too ashamed to repeat.

"You're telling me that you're actually a raccoon shifter?"

"Yes."

"And you don't know *anyone* named Rita Procyon?"

"*No!* I'm Canadian, too. You want to ask me if I know Celine Dion and Seth Rogen too?"

His mouth twisted. He looked like he wanted to say more, to continue his line of questioning, but he seemed to change his mind.

"I'll level with you," he said. "Lilly is my employer. She's a powerful vampire. Normally everything is all right, but if someone steals something from her, then it's good to stay out of her way."

Roquette shivered. She'd sensed the woman was a vampire, but it was another thing to hear it confirmed. "So, another raccoon shifter stole from your boss, and now she wants to start a fight. That it?"

"Something like that," he sighed. "But you're a civilian. You say you don't know anything about this, then fine. I believe you. Still, you have to leave."

"Why, though?" She tried not to assume the worst about vampires, but maybe she should if Lilly was really all that bad. "Is your boss a lunatic or something? She'd just off me because I *look* like someone she hates?"

She'd meant it almost as a joke, half accusing him of making an issue out of something small and insignificant.

However, the way he continued to stare at her, as though silently answering her question, made her stomach drop.

"She's a lunatic?"

"I'm not saying that."

He wasn't *not* saying it either.

"You're saying she'd hurt me if I stuck around."

His mouth twisted into a fine line. "I believe the best course of action would be for you to leave here. As soon as possible."

Which was such a political answer that she had to wonder if he was in the wrong business.

Go back to the party. Ignore this weirdo. Esme is back there, and she's going to help me find my fated mate. The person who will love and accept me, despite my checkered past.

But this guy was standing right here, telling that if she didn't leave right away, something terrible would happen. Possibly to her.

Self-preservation should always be a top priority, and the fact that Roquette hesitated on it really said something. She was so reluctant to leave because she wanted to have a normal life. Wanted to give up all the stealing and wanted to stop feeling lonely.

"Wait, what if I could *help* you and your boss?"

SEVEN

"You said you weren't involved at all. How could you help?" Mr. Sunglasses tilted his head to the side a little, his brows furrowing.

"I... I used to steal, too. When I was younger, and, okay, I was playing into the raccoon stereotype, but it is what it is."

He was still looking at her as though she was off her rocker.

"I had nothing to do with whatever the other raccoon took from your boss, but if I were to help her, would she leave me alone?"

He seemed to be considering it.

"I mean..." Roquette continued. "When I was caught by the police... I agreed to help them. Mostly I had to rat on people so I wouldn't go to prison, and it sucked. I told myself that I would turn over a new leaf. No more stealing. Not even in people's trash bins."

She regretted telling him that the instant it was out of her mouth.

"It was usually the recycling. I tried to keep it clean." She just couldn't stop running her mouth.

He looked like he was having trouble taking all this in. "You were going through people's garbage?"

"I'm a raccoon, all right?" she snapped. "I'm sick of people looking at me like what I do is so weird. Bears like their honey and their salmon. Wolves and dogs chase squirrels. Raccoons dig around in the trash."

Not the noblest of pastimes. Not like the cute rabbit shifters who loved carrot cake or the kitty shifter who chased mice. No. Roquette's animal's thing had to be trash.

In the silence that hovered between them, Roquette heard Danny Devito's voice in her head saying, *I'm the Trash Man!*

And then the corner of Mr. Sunglasses' mouth quirked, which didn't make her feel any better about things.

"Are you laughing at me?"

"A little." He shrugged. "Why go through the trash through? You're not an actual raccoon. I'm sure you could fight the impulse."

"I don't know!" She hated answering that question. "It's just interesting. You see those dark bags or closed bins, and you think... what kind of treasures might be hidden inside? Do you have any idea how much good stuff people throw away?"

He probably didn't care either, but the amount of good furniture, clothes, and even collectibles that she was later able to sell online had been mind-boggling.

As far as she was concerned, people were way too wasteful, and she just had strong impulses to dig for and find the perfectly usable items that lay waiting for her in the receptacles behind the malls.

"Anyway, not that you care, but there are some big box stores that throw away good things that I can repurpose and sell. That's how I made my living. Flipping."

"Flipping?" he asked.

"Yeah, but they ended up getting wise to it. Now they don't throw away anything. Instead, they take all the stuff they couldn't sell, or all the returns they couldn't put back on shelves, and shove it all in boxes and sell it to flippers as *mystery boxes.*"

"Mystery boxes?" Mr. Sunglasses seemed more interested than she would have guessed he would be.

"They're all scams. You can pay fifty to two hundred bucks for a box and end up getting nothing but no-name phone chargers, junk electronics, and slow-selling stuff like socks, notebooks, and light bulbs."

"Oh."

Roquette narrowed her eyes, sensing that maybe he was just humoring her. "I was only explaining so you don't think I was in random home's trash cans. I kept a plan about it, and I wasn't eating anything I took, either."

Not anymore, but she wasn't about to get into *that* with him, either.

The morals, ethics, and art of dumpster diving were lost on too many people, but she was trying to turn a new leaf, at least when it came to the stealing part of her former life.

"Anyway, let me help. If I can get in and do a little spying, then maybe your bossy lady will leave me out of it."

"Or she could assume you're trying to tip off her target. Which you don't want to do."

"I won't!" Roquette objected. "Believe me, I've made mistakes and ended up on the wrong side of shady people before, and I don't want to do it again."

This was definitely shady, and she might be getting in a little over her head, but if she wanted to stick around for Esme's help, what choice did Roquette have?

"You shouldn't be offering this." From behind the dark

sunglasses, his red eye glowed so bright that she could see it burning through the shades.

Roquette shivered.

"I can't leave." Roquette thought about it a little deeper. "I *won't* leave."

His mouth twisted into a crooked line, his nose crinkling. "Is a Christmas party really worth this to you?"

Roquette steeled herself. "I'm not here for the party. I'm here... for Esme."

He didn't say anything. She took that to mean he didn't understand.

Because, of course he didn't. Mr. Sunglasses probably couldn't appreciate feeling so lonely that it hurt or understand how important it was to find someone who wouldn't judge her for everything he'd been smirking over.

"Esme can find anyone their fated mate. It's, like, her gift. I'm here so she can find me... someone. I don't know who they are or what they look like, but we would just be... perfect together."

"Any potential lover you met would just be wasted if you got yourself killed over this."

"*Kill me?* For real?" This man was *not* making a great case for vampires.

"You think I would try kidnapping you because Lilly wanted to say some mean words to you?"

"How do I know? I don't know *anything*. Hell, I don't even know your name!" God, it was getting cold. She wanted to go back to the warmth of the party. She also *really* wanted to tell Harmony that something was definitely up. To warn her.

"My name is Aaron James Smith." He seemed to stand a little taller, if that was even possible. His entire body looked solid and broad, like he could bust through a brick wall if he wanted.

Roquette laughed. "Did you just say your last name is Smith?"

"I did."

"Like, that's your real last name? The one you were born with? You didn't change it? Or just say a fake to be mysterious?"

"It usually works to my advantage if people can't tell if it's real or not, but yes, it's my real name. It's up to you if you believe me or not."

"So, you could be lying?"

"Could be."

She didn't care. Roquette couldn't stop smiling about it either. "Okay, whatever you say, *Agent Smith*."

He frowned, clearly not catching the reference to *The Matrix*. Roquette was all the more delighted by the confusion she sensed beneath those shades.

"Anyway," Smith said. "I've worked for Lilly for the better part of a year, and yes, she would kill without a second thought, for any reason. For no reason, even. Generally, she kills when she feels someone has wronged her. Old family vampires like her are used to doling out their own justice."

"Uh-huh, and you choose to work for someone like that?" Roquette asked. "What if she decides to give you a little justice of your own for giving me the heads up?"

"Well, I *shouldn't* be helping you. The only reason I can even walk right now, or see, is because of her."

EIGHT

THE MECHANICAL EYE SUDDENLY HAD A WHOLE NEW MEANING, AND Roquette found herself staring at his legs. She couldn't see anything beneath his pants, obviously, but knowing there was something other than flesh beneath them....

"You didn't tell me your name," he said, bringing her back from her thoughts.

"I'm Roquette," she said, deciding not to pursue questions about what may or may not have happened to his body.

Now he smiled. "Like Rocket Racoon?"

"*No.* Not like Rocket Racoon." Her parents had not been comic book fans. It had just been an unhappy coincidence that her name sounded so close to that famous damned raccoon. Mostly only the geeks really knew about it until those stupid movies came out. "Like the singer."

"Oh, right," Smith said, nodding vaguely in that way people did when they pretended to know what she was talking about for the sake of politeness.

"You need to listen to me and listen good." Smith, apparently done with the pleasantries, stepped into her personal space, giving Roquette a good feeling for the size of him, reminding her of how powerful his hands had been when he'd grabbed her and tried taking her way.

But his closeness also warmed her up. She honestly wouldn't mind it if he decided to get a little closer.

"Whatever you're looking for, Roquette, you're not going to find it at that party. That woman, Esme, who can supposedly find people their soul mates? Come on. That sounds like new age, scam artist bullshit. You don't need a soul mate. You need to stay alive and safe. Lilly wants revenge on Rita, and she will get it."

"What did Rita take from Lilly?" Roquette asked.

"That's not your concern... or mine," Smith added softly. "The point is, you can go out and find a boyfriend or girlfriend on your own. You're more in control of your life than you think you are, and you don't need to be taken in by someone wanting your money. Trust me. Go meet some nice guy or girl—"

"Guy," she clarified, taken in by the sound of his voice, the determination in his eyes, and honest-to-fucking-God confidence boost he was giving.

A perfect stranger. Giving her the best pep talk she'd ever had in her life.

Roquette was captivated.

"Fine," he sighed. "Guy. Go to some coffee shops and strike up some conversations until you find someone who doesn't mind that you get off on digging in the trash."

"Hey!" she objected, laughing. "It's not a sexual thing!"

He flashed her a smile that made her stomach flutter. "The point is, if he's worth your time, he'll be interesting, he'll pay attention to you, and he'll accept all of your quirks."

Such a mundane and normal idea as finding love in the

local Starbucks terrified her. She'd received too many dirty looks when she revealed that side of herself. Had too many people walk away, too grossed out to listen to her explanations or excuses.

And right about then, Roquette had her second epiphany. "Do you think I'm gross?"

"You don't look gross to me."

Those few little words made her fall half in love with him right there.

Christ, she really *was* desperate, wasn't she?

"Like you said," he continued. "You're not swimming around in broken needles, used baby diapers, and rotting food. The only problem I have with you right now is that you're willing to get into something you don't need to. For the chance of meeting a man? Come on, you're better than that."

He didn't know she was better than that. He was just trying to say all the right things to boost her confidence because he wanted to keep her safe for some reason.

It was kind of sweet.

But the effort was futile.

Smith thought the Baer sisters were full of new age, scam artist bullshit, but Roquette knew better. If Smith wasn't a shifter, then he couldn't possibly understand that shifters had a destiny with *one specific person*. And Esme Baer was absolutely successful in helping people find that mate.

Maybe Smith couldn't relate because he didn't have the same loneliness Roquette had. Perhaps love and a happily-ever-after just weren't something that he felt the need for like she did.

Either way, he wasn't talking her out of returning to the party. It would be one thing to just ghost on Harmony, but a whole other thing to know the sisters might be in danger and not do everything she could to warn her.

Especially because Roquette's nerves around Smith had started to settle, and a new feeling was blooming. And if she were correct on what that sensation meant, then she already owed Esme payment for services rendered.

Roquette needed a different tactic.

"Okay, I'll go home, but on one condition."

"All right, what's that?" Smith didn't look entirely happy, but there was a relieved sag to his shoulders, at least.

"You need to walk me back to the house so I can grab my coat. I need it. It's cold out here, and I'm not leaving it behind."

Beneath the shades, she could see his eye twitching. The non-mechanical one. "I do that, and you will leave?"

"Cross my heart and hope to—"

"Don't finish that. Let's just go, Roquette," he said, sounding very much as though he was calling her *Rocket*, and not *Roquette*.

"Sure thing, and thank you for helping me, *Agent Smith*."

SMITH SEEMED to make it part of his mission to step on her heels as they walked back to the party.

He was hovering, like he was preventing anyone from getting between them.

It would have been cute, had her Achilles tendon not been killing her after the fifth time he scraped his shoe on the back of her heel.

They barely got to the door when she whirled around

on him. *"Will you cut that out?"* She hissed. "That fucking hurts."

She could tell she'd shocked him. "My apologies. Let's just get this over with."

Luckily, he didn't know where the coatroom was, so Roquette could walk with confidence back to the main room and head straight toward the big tree where she'd first found Harmony that night.

The party was still full of people chatting and drinking idly. Enjoying themselves and having nothing to do with the stupid drama of Smith, Lilly, and Rita. Roquette looked from one side of the room to the other, looking for Harmony's wild mass of orange curls and coming up empty.

Roquette looked back to where Smith was keeping a few feet of distance. She noticed that his calm, cool exterior he'd put on outside had disappeared.

Now, he looked almost... awkward, glancing around himself, waiting for someone to realize he wasn't dressed in proper Christmas party attire.

Or maybe he was waiting for Lilly to jump out and attack at any moment.

He looked her way, and even with the shades on, it was clear he'd caught her staring.

Why did she feel all fluttery as he closed the distance between them? He probably wanted her to feel intimidated, but the joy in the room, combined with the drunken people who were now singing along with the Christmas music, made her feel like if she looked up, she might see mistletoe.

But he quickly killed her vibe when he gruffly asked, "Why are you just standing there?"

"Uh," Roquette had to look away for a second to compose herself, totally not getting all shivery over the sound of his gruff voice.

"You're here for a jacket, and that's all, remember?"

"Hey! None of this!" A man, half in the bag, his cheeks flushed with color and a broad smile on his face, looped an arm around Smith's neck and shoulder. "Come on, man! It's a happy time here for everyone. You should be—*gah!*"

The noise he made would have been funny if it hadn't been caused by Smith grabbing his wrist and twisting.

Hard.

The poor man was forced down to his knees with a sharp cry as the pressure became too much.

And Smith growled at him, white teeth flashing as he snarled, "Don't ever touch me again."

Roquette didn't need to see Smith's eyes to understand the level of rage he felt at that moment. There were other obvious tells for anger that shifters could pick up on. Starting with the scent change and moving on to the way his brows shot together and his nostrils flared.

Smith was getting ready to take a bite out of the man.

It was frightening to look at, and Roquette wasn't the only one who stared.

The chatter around them quieted, though the happy Christmas jingle continued to play, giving the whole room a thick, awkward vibe.

Roquette had to do something. She stepped forward, pressing her hand to Smith's shoulder. "Hey, come on. I'm sure he didn't mean anything by it."

"Is everything all right over here?"

Roquette looked up. The woman who'd greeted her, Emily, and her fiancée Mark had approached them, looking all too ready to kick out the person injuring other guests.

Maybe they'd call the cops.

Part of Roquette thought that, well, all things considered, maybe they *should* call the cops.

But if there really was an evil vampire chick out there looking to cause trouble, how much damage could she cause before the police even got there?

"We're good. Just a misunderstanding." Roquette grabbed Smith's shoulder. Through the suit, it felt cold and hard, like she was holding onto steel.

And she was reminded of how tightly he'd gripped her while yanking her away from the house.

She had no doubt that he could overpower her if he really wanted to. He could probably easily break the guy's arm no matter what Roquette, Emily, or Mark had to say about it.

So when he let go of the man, Roquette felt it had more to do with his own self-control than any effect she may have had on him.

Except he looked right at her, and she could swear she could see his eyes through those heavy shades.

The mechanical one glowed.

"My friend here doesn't like being touched," Roquette said lamely, not having a smoother explanation ready.

The guy Smith had assaulted jumped up to his feet. His tipsy, flush-faced, easy-going stature had melted into something that looked a little more ready to brawl.

He didn't fight, though. Even with some drinks in him, it seemed the guy thought better of it as he rubbed at his wrist and elbow.

Roquette was pretty sure he was lucky Smith hadn't broken it.

She gripped Smith a little tighter, pulling him away from the scene before someone really did whip out their phone and call the police.

The chatter slowly started back up. Not everyone in the party had seen what happened, but soon everyone would know to stay away from the guy in the sunglasses, and that wasn't going to help their little plan to keep things on the down low.

"What is your problem?" she hissed. "You can't just do that."

Smith didn't say anything. He simply set his mouth in a firm line and rolled his shoulders.

"Are you serious?" she cried. "All that because he stuck his arm around you?"

"I didn't like it."

She didn't understand. "I'm touching you right now."

"That's different." They came to a stop near the staircase, and Smith looked down at her, then away. "This is useless. Please just gather your jacket and leave."

She felt bad for him. Clearly, he was afraid of his boss, the vampire, Lilly.

But Roquette had a mission, now. A certainty she'd

never felt before swelled inside her. The knowledge that this was something she needed to do, and she wouldn't rest until it was complete.

It wouldn't go away. Just like every time a delicious-looking trash bin caught her eye. It was something that couldn't be ignored. She would have to poke and prod her way through it.

"No," she said to Smith, straightening her shoulders and standing as tall as she could.

Smith's entire body went rigid.

Roquette knew she was on thin ice, but her compulsion to help the Baers wouldn't go away. It intensified, even as Smith stared down at her in such an intimidating way.

She repeated herself and took it up a notch. "No, fuck you. I'm not leaving."

Smith stepped right up to her, until they were toe-to-toe, reminding her of his height and size. "Do you really think there will be any mercy for you if—"

"I. Don't. Care." Roquette said, punctuating her words. "What are you going to do? You can't drag me off again. We're in a room full of people who will see you and stop you."

"I told you what danger you're in."

"Why do you care? It doesn't seem like you care about any of these other people who might be in harm's way when your crazy girlfriend—boss, whatever—starts exacting her revenge plan. So, I appreciate the concern you've shown for *me*, but *I* care about the others. *I'm* going to warn the Baers."

"Then don't expect me to step in and save you." Smith's voice was low, threatening, and Roquette didn't think it had anything to do with his need to keep his voice down while the rest of the guests enjoyed the music and conversation. "I've stood back and watched Lilly hurt plenty of people, in ways you can't imagine. I will absolutely let her tear you apart if she gets her hands on you. Don't think for one second that I won't."

That was just the thing. She didn't believe him.

She didn't know this guy. She really had no reason to trust him, besides the fact that he said he was trying to protect her.

But the more and more she poked at the attraction growing inside her, the more confident she became that it was *the feeling*. Not that she hadn't ruled out the fact that her loneliness might be fooling her into believing that this man was her mate—desperation had caused her to feel much stranger things.

It's not like she'd ever experienced meeting her *fated mate* before.

Still, she also had no proof that she *was* completely off base in thinking Esme had put her in the right place at the right time to meet Smith on purpose.

Which meant Esme had fulfilled her end of the deal, and Roquette owed her a solid.

Whether or not her presumed fated mate intended on watching his boss gut her like a fish.

"You want your vampire friend to hurt me and everyone in here? Why don't you just call her over?" Roquette taunted.

"Stop that."

"I mean, you got me right here. I couldn't run away from you if I tried."

"Will you shut up?"

"Just get her over here, and she can start the questioning—torture—whatever it is, and she can take her revenge against the people who stole from her."

The glow of his mechanical eye grew more prominent now. Roquette could really see it glowing beneath the shades.

She was definitely pushing the buttons of someone dangerous. Why?

A sliver of... something... pulsed through her. Not fear, and not entirely unease.

And for some stupid reason, that sliver of whatever turned her on.

Fuck my life.

TEN

Roquette waited, but he said nothing. He didn't attack her as he did the guy who'd wrapped his arm around Smith's shoulders. He didn't yell at her or tell her she was an idiot either.

The crinkle in his brow did deepen through. Definitely a sign he was glaring.

Smith was probably trying to melt her face with that stare beneath the shades.

She didn't *think* his mechanical eye had the ability to actually do that... not that she could tell whether or not it was equipped with lasers. It wasn't like she was some kind of tech genius who could assess something like that from a distant visual inspection.

She only assumed it was void of offensive modes because if it *could* attack, Smith would have at least tried it as a scare tactic at some point already.

"What do you care?" he demanded, his voice a soft but dangerous growl. "You really value the lives of these *strangers* over your own? You think any of them would do the same for you? And all because you came here to get this Esme woman to find something for you?"

Someone, but she didn't correct him. "Yeah..."

"That is a stupid thing to die for."

That cut her in a way it shouldn't have.

Though the feeling inside of her still grew for him, the more he spoke, the more her brain told her she was an idiot for even entertaining the idea that he might be *the one...*

He was an ass. *And I'm only feeling funny toward him because he's saying all this 'protector' garbage, and it's preying on my lonely heart.*

Whatever. That was neither here nor there. The point was that the opinion of a stranger shouldn't affect her the way they did.

But she was a sucker for punishment, it seemed, because even as he hurt her, she couldn't help but want to dig her feet in a little more. To confront him with the fact that she wasn't going anywhere.

"You don't get to judge my motivations. You work for a psychopath who is ready to kill someone for *looking* like someone she dislikes. So fuck right off with that holier-than-though bullshit."

His head remained still, but Roquette had gotten used to seeing the red glow through his sunglasses. He was trying to act nonchalant, but his eye was darting around, making sure no one could hear what she was saying.

Luckily the music and chatter were too loud, and no one seemed to be overhearing their conversation.

He didn't want anyone hearing her?

Too damn bad for him.

"So, in conclusion, I'm not going anywhere."

"Why are you doing this to me?" he hissed. "I stuck my neck out for you, dragging you away from the party and giving you the truth about my boss, and this is how I'm repaid for it. I should have never..."

"Why did you do it, then?" she asked, throwing his words back at him. "From what you're saying, you're ready to watch her take out as many people as she'd like, so why did you go behind your boss's back to help me... Someone who is a stranger to you?"

She saw it again, the intensifying glow of his mechanical eye behind the shades, followed by the deep crinkle of his brow.

He looked furious.

But for someone who supposedly worked for a killer in heels, he didn't do anything toward her to shut her up or drag her out. He didn't abandon her, either.

He just pushed the sunglasses up a touch, pinching the bridge between his eyes as he heaved a heavy sigh.

Her confidence wavered, and she started to consider that maybe she shouldn't be enjoying messing with him so much. Whatever his reason *was* for helping her, it was neither here nor there. Because clearly, he was bothered by the idea of harm coming to her.

No. She shouldn't feel sorry for him. It was all his own damned fault, really. He was the one who worked for a monster.

"It's not that simple," he said, finally. "Would it answer all of your questions If I told you that seeing you triggered something in me? That the moment I saw you, I was intrigued, and when Lilly said she was going to kill you, everything inside of me screamed to not let that happen?"

Why couldn't Roquette live in the kind of world where she could actually buy it when guys said stuff like that? No... she knew Smith was laying it on too thick, trying to tell her what he thought she might respond to. It was a reasonable assumption, too, since she'd made no secret of the fact that she was there to find love.

Hopefully he didn't also know that she'd kind of developed something of a crush on him already.

"Right, okay, yep, sure," she said, rolling her eyes. "So I'm the one person in the world you care about. You'll save me, but everyone else? To hell with them." Roquette gestured broadly to the people in the room around her.

Roquette found herself struggling against the urge to rip his sunglasses off his face. She wanted to look him in the good eye. She wanted him to show all his features while he told her such mean lies about having feelings for her.

Instead, he grabbed her arm and pulled her closer to him. "Or maybe I wish I could save them all, but I can't. Maybe there's nothing I can do about it, but for you—for the one stubborn misfit raccoon that I had the poor fortune to cross paths with—I'd risk everything. Maybe if I'd known you would have been so opposed to being rescued, then I would have made a better choice."

And then it dawned on her.

Smith wasn't there, with Lilly, willingly. He didn't like working for a murderer. But he wasn't free to walk away.

Not only that, but his vampire psychopath boss wasn't stupid. She already knew he'd helped Roquette! She'd probably been watching them the whole time. Maybe she would have followed them into the woods if she hadn't been busy working on her revenge plan.

And if she really was as bad as Smith made her out to be, Lilly would make Smith pay for helping Roquette. Would she kill him? Or would she punish him in other ways because he was some kind of superweapon that she couldn't afford to lose?

Roquette gulped, wondering—and hoping it wasn't the

case—if his metal and mechanical enhancements were the results of those kinds of punishments.

"Look, you're already screwed, I see that now," Roquette said, her words emerging faster and faster as the excitement built up inside of her.

Everything was making total and complete sense.

Smith had tried to save Roquette that night... but Harmony had invited Roquette to the party that night to save *him*.

I know it. That has *to be why Harmony wanted me here tonight.*

"Smith, it's time for you to break the ties that bind, you know?" Roquette reached out and grabbed both his hands, feeling joyful enough that she almost bounced on her toes. "We crossed paths for a reason, and now I know why. But in the same way that you were just begging me to make a run for it to save myself, it's now my turn to ask you for the same."

"I don't understand..." Smith blinked at her in confusion, but he didn't pull his hands away from hers.

In fact, his warm human thumb caressed the back of her hand, sending a tingle through her.

Maybe he hadn't lied about having feelings for me.

She couldn't think about that now, though. She had a mission, and her cyborg-man looked like he was just about convinced to join her in it.

"Smith, there's one way you and I *both* walk out of here alive tonight, okay? And that's if we work together."

CHAPTER

ELEVEN

"Alright," Smith said, wetting his lips though his brows still pulled together in the glare that told Roquette he wasn't happy about the situation. "I'll help you."

Actually, he was helping himself, but that was alright. Roquette wouldn't debate semantics with him. She could do it later, since they'd have a lifetime for her to rub it all in.

"Good choice." Roquette smiled up at him, squeezing his hand tightly. "So, I think we should start with finding my look-alike."

"Rita Procyon," Smith said, clearing his throat and finally pulling his hands back as he surveyed the room for the person he spoke of. "The man she's with, Dallas Bordeaux, will know who Lilly Saint James is. I'm sure they will react accordingly once they spot her."

He spoke without looking at Roquette, and the pair of them began making their way through the giant house, holding hands.

Not because they were trying to look like a couple, Roquette figured, but because it would make losing each other in this enormous house with such a giant crowd much harder.

She felt like she was getting ready to go on an old-fashioned Nancy Drew Mystery mission.

There was so much she didn't know about. So many questions she still had.

Namely... "How did you get wrapped up with this woman if she's such a lunatic? I mean, if she wants to hurt people just for looking like the people who wronged her, isn't that someone you should steer clear of?"

Smith barely glanced back at her as he deftly avoided other party-goers who tried to shove drinks at him.

Clearly, they were the people who didn't know he'd nearly broken someone's arm already.

"She... saved my life."

That was enough to make Roquette nearly pause, and she might have stopped moving entirely had he not kept such a steady grip on her hand.

"Seriously?"

Even with the shades on, it was apparent he was rolling his eyes. "Why would I lie about something like that?"

The question caught Roquette off guard. "I don't know. It just seemed..." She didn't have an answer for what it seemed like. Too dramatic? Too unbelievable?

She didn't say it aloud, though, since literally anything she said could be used against her. She didn't want the guy who worked with a dangerous vampire lady to think she was making fun of him.

So she finally settled on, "How did she save your life?"

Smith snapped his head toward her and stared. Finally, with slow, deliberate movement, he brought his hand up and lifted the sunglasses just slightly off his nose. Just enough for her to see his eyes.

Not that she really needed to see them. She'd already had a good look at the glowing ball he called an eye when she'd knocked his sunglasses off in the woods.

But seeing it again, really taking in the scar tissue that surrounded both the mechanical eye and the natural one, unsettled her in a way she hadn't felt before. She was, after all, focused on trying to run away from him when he was free of the sunglasses in the forest.

But now, she yearned to reach out and gently stroke the scars while she could only imagine what had done that to him.

She didn't have to wonder for long since he answered the question she didn't ask. "I was serving a client—on my own, when I worked for myself. Protection only. I took acid to my eyes for that client, and I'm lucky this one still works as well as it does."

He tapped the side of his face that still had the functioning eye. Then, dropping the sunglasses back into place, he patted his shoulder. "Took a gunshot to my shoulder and elbow that same day."

Roquette swallowed. "Who... Jesus, who were you protecting?"

"That's classified and not at all important to your original question."

Christ, he was clinical.

"The point is that my client refused to pay more than he was contracted for when it came to medical. I don't entirely blame him. It was my own fault for not putting it into the contract I had him sign, but after taking acid to my face and multiple bullets to my arm and back, I thought the rich bastard would help me."

Roquette nodded. She would have thought the same

thing. Anyone who saved her life would get whatever they wanted out of her.

At least, that's easy enough to think, but a bit different in practice. Smith had, after all, said he was saving her earlier, but she'd staunchly refused.

And she was insisting on making things as difficult as possible for him.

You're saving us both, she reminded herself.

"So... your boss, Lilly, paid your medical bills? And offered you a new arm and eye? A... mechanical one? Were they needed to save your life? I mean, was everything that life-threatening?"

She regretted the question the instant it was out of her mouth.

Smith didn't look overly offended, but that didn't mean he wasn't hiding something, letting it simmer beneath the surface.

He would be very good at hiding things if the glowing in his eye didn't intensify every time she said something that bothered him.

"If you're suddenly faced with the idea that your career is over because you're missing an arm and a limb, you might find yourself willing to accept a crazy person's offer to fix you. So yes, she absolutely saved my life. I owe it to her, and I've gone behind her back now for *you.*"

He said it like it was an accusation.

"Are you... changing your mind?" Roquette asked.

The air around them was way too damned cheery, all things considered. There was too much... sparkly, happy, sugary bullshit all around them for the tension between them to be as charged as it was.

"No." He kept looking at her, though, like he wanted to say something else.

Roquette waited for it, but it didn't come. Instead, he dropped her hand and stormed past her, heading up the stairs.

She followed him.

The sound of the music quieted the further away they went from the main party, but the hum of it pushed through the floor.

"So, that arm that grips as hard as a vice... it's metal?"

He glanced back at her, checking each door they came across. Most were unlocked, and he had a glance inside each.

"Yes." He raised his arm, not looking back at her. "This is a biomechatronic prosthetic Lilly paid for. Very advanced."

"And strong," Roquette said, recalling what it felt like when he'd grabbed her.

After opening another door, Smith stopped and really looked at her. "I do apologize. It wasn't my intention to make you fearful or to cause pain."

She forced a smile, trying to get over the angsty backstory that made her heart clench for him. "It's fine. You were trying to protect me. That's your job, right? Or was, rather... to protect people?"

He turned away as though embarrassed. "Used to be." He peeked his head into the next room. "There are bags in here."

He stepped into the room, and Roquette followed. The bed had been perfectly made, but there were some bags by the window. A brown duffel bag and a small suitcase.

"I guess this place probably rents out rooms, huh?" Roquette surmised.

"Probably."

"Should we be in here?" Roquette stepped inside and

closed the door behind her, ignoring her own advice. "Whoever is renting it might not like us being in here."

With hardly a care in the world, Smith walked right up to the bags and began opening them like they belonged to him.

The way he pilfered through the clothes and toiletries spoke to the little raccoon thief inside of her, and she piqued up, intently watching him skillfully work.

He was very thorough, being just careful enough to not make it obvious that he was disturbing everything.

She couldn't take it any longer. She had to know what he was seeing inside those bags.

CHAPTER

TWELVE

She stepped in closer, getting to her knees and feeling grave disappointment when she saw the bags held only clothes—why not a bag of money or jewels for once?

"What are you looking for?"

"Identification. Pictures. Something with a name on it."

"Because you think this is Rita and Dallas' room? Why?"

"Because they weren't heading this way to attend a party. We believe they were heading here to meet up with the Baer sisters and perhaps find some sort of protection under them." Smith kept on looking, so focused, pulling out every pocket he could, checking every sleeve before carefully folding everything and placing it back.

The clothes did look like they belonged to a man and a woman. The men's clothes were in the duffel, while the woman's clothing came from the suitcase.

The more Roquette looked, the more excited she became. "Looks like you've got a knack for this work, much like I do. The pilfering, I mean."

"This is not the trash or the recycling."

"Yeah, but it's still going through someone else's shit."

She picked up a lacy bra that would have been too small for her to wear. Not knowing why, but maybe feeling a little adventurous, she brought it up to her chest. "You think the color suits me?"

She didn't think he would actually crack a smile at her, but he did. It was there, and it was so adorable compared to the cold exterior she'd known so far that it took her breath away for a few seconds.

"You're ridiculous." He said, his voice surprisingly full of mirth.

"Ridiculous in a good way, though?"

"Yes, a good way. We'll leave it at that," he said, then growled, shaking his head. "I don't think this belongs to the people we're looking for."

"How can you tell?"

Smith patted his arm, the one that felt like steel. "Keeping the... new and improved parts of yourself requires some... maintenance from time to time. Nothing drastic, but a small kit of tools, a cleaning kit, some oils, those are usually helpful."

"Oh." Then it dawned on her. "*Oh!* Dallas is like you?"

Smith nodded in confirmation, and Roquette looked back at the bags. Yeah, nothing that suggested the owners were doing any kind of regular mechanical maintenance.

"I guess it was a long shot anyway."

"We'll keep looking," Smith said, zipping the bags back up. He stood, looked at her, then around the room like he would find the right answer somewhere in there.

Then another realization hit her. "Woah, wait... Dallas is like you, and you said he'd know who Lilly was... so that means that... wait... Dallas is with Rita, and Lilly is mad Rita took something of hers... is it Dallas? She's mad that Rita took Dallas! Was he Lilly's boyfriend or something?"

"No, Dallas wasn't *with* Lilly in that way." Smith looked away from her, and she got the impression he was rolling his eyes.

"Don't do that to me, Bot Boy."

"Bot Boy?"

She ignored his question on the nickname. "Okay, when I had offered to help, I thought it was something I could help her get *back*. Like, a physical item. I thought when you said that something was stolen, or whatever, that we were talking about regular trash panda stuff."

"Regular trash panda stuff?"

"Stop repeating me. You know what I mean. This is insane. I mean, it's not like Dallas is being held against his will, right? He willingly chose to be with Rita?"

Smith didn't answer her. He looked as though he was trying to figure out what he was supposed to say at all.

Roquette didn't like that. It gave her time to think.

Her stupid brain made a lot of guesses, and there was one set of guesses that she was pretty sure were lining up just nicely.

"You said you work for this woman because you owe her? How many other people has she done this for?"

"You're in way over your head."

"I don't care. You work for a crazy woman who wants to hurt me for just looking like someone else."

"You've never even met her."

"I know her well enough to know that she is so fucked up that you're breaking rank, or whatever, to help me get out of whatever it is she would do to me if she got me. I also know that she's got more than one cybernetically enhanced battle bot man on her team willing to dole out destruction on her orders."

"You're making it sound like something it's not. We're

people that she's helped, and we owe her. We're not robots..."

"But you kind of are if she makes your decisions for you," Roquette said sadly. She didn't want to rub it in his face, but she needed him to see the truth. "And Dallas... he ran away with Rita to escape Lilly, that's it, isn't it?"

It was the same scenario she was in with Smith. She felt sick, and she clenched her fist to her stomach, trying to keep that terrible feeling at bay.

"Dallas made a deal with Lilly and is refusing to keep it," Smith said bitterly.

"Like you?"

He paused. "Exactly like me."

"Uh-huh. So neither of you are the sort of guys who want some crazy bitch hurting people—let alone to help her do it. So he took the opportunity to flee when it came to him."

"You don't know that."

"No, but if it's true, then it makes you and him really similar to each other, right?"

Smith pressed his lips together. She'd struck a nerve.

"How much do you actually know about this stuff?" she asked, needing to know. "Do you really know every detail about the guy your boss has a hard-on for?"

People typically didn't like it when she used crude language like that, but she didn't care to fight it now. Let the discomfort begin. She could use it to distract herself from the very bad, very improper thoughts she was having about a dangerous, handsome, tormented cyber guy she hardly knew.

Smith's hands clenching to fists wasn't the best sign in the world, but she figured it meant she was getting something through to him.

She hoped, anyway.

"I do as I'm told," Smith bit out the words. "Dallas was supposed to do the same. It's as simple as that."

"Because Lilly saved your life?"

"Yes."

"And his?"

"That's not my business or yours."

He was so fucking handsome, but the more he talked, the more stupid she thought him to be.

"You don't know anything about this guy, do you?" Roquette guessed. "This isn't some brother soldier you worked with. Wait, did you even *know* that you weren't her only robo-soldier?"

He didn't answer.

"So you walk up to Dallas, and he's going to know instantly that you're not on team cyborg freedom. That you're here on Lilly's behest, chasing him down because you were told to."

"Be quiet."

"But you *are* team freedom now, right? Cause you said you were already screwed from helping me in the first place. I'm guessing there's no going back now. Unless you think apprehending Dallas and delivering him and Rita to Lilly will garner you some favor—"

"I said *be quiet.*" He grabbed her by her shoulder, pushing her against the nearest wall while leaning in close, his chest pressed against hers, the warmth of his breath ghosting across her face and making her entire body shiver with goosebumps and newfound life.

Life she'd never felt before. As though she were a virgin and had never had a man pressing up against her.

"You talk *far too much,*" he snarled. The danger in his

voice and in how he pressed against her had Roquette's body reacting in ways she didn't anticipate.

Especially when he stopped snarling, his face softened, and he just kept staring.

Granted, she didn't think he meant for the moment to become anything sexual, but that was too damn bad for him.

She was totally taking this to be a sexual thing. Maybe Smith was just as horny and frustrated as she was and had the same confusing attraction toward her that she had toward him.

The fact that made it worse was how he just… stood there. Holding her, his body against hers, lips so close that if she tilted her head at the right angle, she might just end up kissing him.

"Well?" she asked, half daring him to do something already. "What is it? You're in this thing with me now, or you're planning a double-cross?"

"I've already told you I wanted to protect you."

"But what you want isn't necessarily what you'll do in the end."

The fact that he didn't reply right away told her that she was right on the money. He had an internal conflict happening, and neither of them knew how it would resolve itself.

Which left her with one choice.

She did something bad that, for once, didn't have anything to do with digging around in someone else's recycling bin.

She leaned up and kissed Smith full on the mouth, enjoying how the action took his stuck-up breath away.

CHAPTER

THIRTEEN

She'd shocked him. She felt it.

Even with those stupid sunglasses on, she could see the way his brows shut up to his hairline.

Plus, he didn't breathe.

Did she actually take his breath away? The idea alone had her brimming with all kinds of confidence.

Roquette felt sexy. She felt in *control*. And she felt that it would be super fun to put her arms around his lower back and pull him closer to see how he would react.

God, he was a wall of solid muscle. His body was hot. And he was definitely not pushing her away or making a break for it.

Because he wanted this.

As much as she did.

His mouth went soft against hers, and his tongue probed gently against her lips. Roquette opened for him. She moaned as he slid his tongue against hers.

He tasted like sweet coffee. Cream and sugar.

She fucking *loved* it, pushing her fingers into his short dark hair and gripping tight.

This was a Christmas party, and people hooked up at these sorts of things all the time, right? Granted, she was only *assuming* that Smith was the man Esme wanted her to be with... and if she was wrong, that might make things a bit awkward, but hell... She was going to put all those thoughts out of her mind and have a little bit of sponta- neous fun for once.

Roquette was pretty sure she had never been this horny for someone. It must've been the danger of the situation. Or the fact that it was at a party, in a room rented by strangers.

With this specific guy...

Everything was coming together to make her hot and bothered, and something needed to be done about that right the fuck now.

Which meant that her hands got a little exploratory and she pushed and pulled against his shirt and belt.

Untucking the button down. Fingers fumbled with the belt. The tie could stay. She liked a man in a tie.

She kind of hoped he would tie her up with it.

But maybe they wouldn't have time for that.

His large hands clasped her smaller wrists, stopping her. "Don't."

She froze. Roquette looked up at him, and through the sunglasses, she could see his mechanical eye glowing.

"Don't?"

He shook his head. "If you keep doing that, I'm not gonna be able to stop."

That confused her because it was definitely the point of what she was doing.

"I don't want to stop." She looked at him good and hard. "Do you?"

He pressed his lips together, looking both like he

wanted to say something and also not say it at the same time.

In the end, Roquette couldn't stand it anymore. She reached up and gently took the sunglasses off his face.

The fact that he tried to turn away from her kind of hurt.

Roquette had no idea what she was doing or why, but she placed her hands on his face and forced him to look at her.

He didn't fight her.

He was giving in to what she wanted.

But he still wouldn't meet her eyes.

"You know," Roquette whispered huskily. "For a guy who tries to come off as such a badass, you're kind of shy, aren't you?"

His answering glare might have concerned her an hour or so ago, but now, Roquette felt victorious. Like each moment she was with him, she was digging for clues about him, and the deeper she went, the more shimmery, golden treasures she found.

"This isn't what we should be doing right now," he finally replied.

She pushed her fingers through his hair. The urge to touch everywhere she could reach coursed through her, and it felt like she was helpless against the feeling.

So she did as it commanded her.

"I do a lot of things I'm not supposed to," she replied, staring at him, transfixed.

There was no stopping her. His lips were right there, pink and full. Such a nice mouth for a man. It wasn't fair.

So she kissed him again.

He closed his eyes.

The fact that she could almost see the glow of his red

one from beneath a closed lid should have been distracting, but it wasn't.

She just wanted to touch more of him, to taste more of that coffee taste, and to indulge in what was directly beneath it.

Him.

Roquette was right. She had to be. This was what she was here for.

For Aaron James Smith.

Her hands gripped his forearms, but he didn't push her away. She got the feeling he was considering it, even as he kissed her, but he pulled her closer instead, her chest pressing up against his.

The grip of his one arm was definitely stronger than the other. Painfully so.

She would have ignored it, but it was too much, and Roquette found herself grunting and pushing him back.

He seemed to realize what the problem was, and he let her go. "Sorry. I..."

His mouth set into a hard line, and he abruptly spun around and headed for the door.

"Where are you going?" Roquette ran after him, pushing the door shut just as he opened it.

"This is a mistake. We need to forget this all. I need to go back to Lilly and do my job."

She blinked, and though she should have felt baited by his threat, she grinned. She'd learned his tactics well enough at this point to know that he closed off when she was getting too close to what he really wanted. "Well, I wouldn't say kissing you was a waste of time or anything. I thought it was productive."

"This isn't a game."

"Because your boss is dangerous. I believe you." Not

looking away from him, Roquette flipped the lock on the door. Not exactly trapping him inside, but definitely letting him know she wasn't done with him.

He looked at her, and at the door. His green and red eyes wide. "You are unreal. You don't have any clue what you're dealing with."

"So? If it's that bad, then why shouldn't we live for just a moment?"

She glanced down at his tented pants.

He growled at her. He actually *growled*.

But that didn't disguise the blush she could clearly see forming across his cheeks.

"This isn't a game."

"I'm not playing." And she wasn't. Roquette had never felt so needy before in her life. Definitely not for a guy she'd just met.

She started stripping.

Smith's jaw dropped, and his eyes widened as though he were absolutely scandalized. "Are you kidding me right now?"

She stopped with her hands behind her back, pushing her breasts out toward him. "Does it look like I'm kidding?"

His nostrils flared. He glanced to the door, then back to her, and when she jiggled her boobs a bit, he exhaled hard.

As if he'd been holding that back for a while now.

"Fuck it," he said, grabbing her.

She wrapped her arms around his neck, and when he lifted her off her feet, she curled her legs around his waist.

Finally.

Finally.

CHAPTER

FOURTEEN

When Smith swooped her into his arms, Roquette felt all kinds of adventurous and sexy.

He moved her to the bed. The comforter was plush and soft underneath them as Smith fell down on top of her, kissing her hard and passionately.

They were christening someone else's sleeping space. Any other time, Roquette might have felt a little bad about it, but not right then.

The only thing going through her mind was a solid wall of *yes, yes, yes, yes*.

She still had her pants on, but the shoes had been kicked off somewhere between her shirt hitting the floor and her ass hitting the bed. As Smith pressed against her, she gripped his waist tightly with her thighs and moaned softly when she felt the bulge of his cock against her sex.

Even with some clothes still on, she shivered. The friction was already incredible.

The fact that Smith was breathing hard against her neck, like he was struggling to keep himself in check, made her feel even better.

She was doing this to him. It felt like she had a power over him that was going straight to her head.

Better than the first time she'd ever gone dumpster diving. Like she was being level ten naughty now.

And just like that first time she found a mint-condition collectible exclusive, she wanted to keep going, because there was definitely something amazing to be found here.

"We'll be quick," he said against her throat.

She smiled, nodding. "Okay."

Roquette knew they couldn't exactly have hours and hours of sex when the real world—including a potential murderess—was waiting outside, but she would make the most of the time she had, even if it killed her.

"You're wearing too much," she said, pushing at the overcoat he wore, trying to get to the layers beneath.

He pulled back abruptly.

At first, Roquette thought it was because her hand had brushed against the holster that held his gun.

She hadn't been surprised to find it there. He was, after all, some kind of hitman or something. She'd intended on just ignoring it, but it would make sense that he wouldn't want her touching it. Maybe he didn't trust her not to take it and try hurting him with it.

But no, his hands didn't move to the holster. His hand gripped his tie like he was trying to keep it as straight and pristine as possible.

"You don't want me naked," he said with a tight and uncomfortable grin.

"What?"

He kept smiling at her, leaning in, his warm breath ghosting across her collarbone. "I think you'd like it if I fucked you like this. You naked, me with my clothes on. Fast and fun, what do you say?"

She shivered. "It sounds like a good time." It might sound better for him to be naked too, but they could work on his comfort level at a later date. If they didn't get on with it soon, they could be discovered and the whole moment lost.

"Good."

"Wait," she said, her rational mind catching up to her lust-filled one. She grabbed Smith's hands and stopped him. "You're hiding something."

"I need to stay dressed. I'm not taking everything off, so I end up unarmed if someone bursts in here." This time, she believed the sexy little growl in his voice.

That made sense, but she got the feeling it wasn't just about staying ready for a potential fight.

It was like he was trying to avoid being an entirely different kind of vulnerable.

Roquette looked into his eyes, really staring at the glowing red one and the scars all around it. He kept it covered most of the time, and now he was keeping his arm covered too.

What else did he feel like he had to hide?

Smith held still as her legs slid up and down his thighs.

One side of him felt a little... harder... colder than the other. One side of him was hard hot muscle, but the other was harder, smoother, thinner...

Lilly gave him an eye, an arm, and apparently a leg too.

Roquette might feel an uneasy loyalty to the person who did that for her, too.

"What happened to you?" she whispered, her damn curiosity overriding her desperate need to get laid.

She regretted the question the instant it was out of her mouth.

He'd already told her that he'd been attacked with acid and bullets. It should have been enough of an answer.

But everyday protection jobs didn't put people in those kinds of situations. What had he *really* been doing?

He didn't pull away. Smith didn't look disgusted with her question either.

He just looked... sad.

"Nothing that I should be getting into." He blinked his eyes again, the red glow of the mechanical eye increasing as he suddenly took on a more predatory air. "I'd rather get into *you* instead."

Oh, okay, wow. There was no way Roquette was going to say no to that.

She brushed her fingers through his hair, grinning up at him, pleased with herself for not ruining the mood. "By all means. I'm kind of over all the talking," she said.

That seemed to be the right thing to say because Smith kissed her hard. He kissed her like he'd been waiting to kiss her since he first laid his eyes on her.

Roquette wanted to keep touching. She wanted to keep exploring. He might want to keep his clothes on, but that didn't mean she had to stop her hands from moving, from trying to get under his shirt.

He wasn't going to get out of this without his clothes rumpled, that was for damned sure.

"Fuck, wait," he growled, pulling back and taking off his overcoat.

Yes!

The holster went next. He was actually wearing a couple of them, to her shock. She hadn't noticed that. One was clearly for his gun. The other seemed to be holding a few knives.

That should have unnerved her, but it didn't.

He tossed them to the side of the bed, right within reach, and nothing else came off.

"I don't want you hurting yourself."

"You're not worried I could hurt you?"

"No."

Okay, ouch. Roquette wasn't entirely loving the idea that he thought of her as a non-threat.

But then his mouth was on hers again, and when she pushed her hands beneath his shirt, untucking it and seeking out skin, Roquette decided that later would be a better time to make him eat his words.

God, his tongue was so nice inside her mouth. That adventurous feeling inside her blew up even though she was the one beneath him, and Roquette wanted to have a turn to dominate.

CHAPTER

FIFTEEN

Roquette pushed her tongue back against Smith's, licking him, pressing to his mouth. He seemed surprised, but he let her do as she wanted, his mechanical hand holding tightly to the back of her neck.

There was a thrill that came with the idea that he could really hurt her if he wanted to, or even if he wasn't careful. He'd gripped her arm a little too tight before, and that had been painful. She wasn't entirely sure if he had a robot arm or if it was made of metal or whatever, but she could tell it was tough.

He didn't hurt her now, but the thrill was still there.

Along with the stupid desire to push him to his limits.

Roquette felt wild and free. She pulled at his belt buckle, unclasping it before letting her hand slide beneath the waist of his pants and boxers, finding his cock.

He gasped for breath when her fingers brushed across the hard length of him. She hadn't even taken him in hand yet, and he was shuddering.

She grinned up at him, their mouths parting, but that

feeling of being alive and in control and sexy came back to her.

She loved being a raccoon. She loved feeling naughty and bad, but feeling sexy was a little harder, in either form. No one thought of trash pandas as sex kittens.

But Smith sure as hell made her feel like one.

His mouth, his beautiful, hot, scorching mouth, moved away from her lips, to her jaw, and down her throat before he began sucking and biting. Like he was trying to mark her in a hurry.

Right. Of course. She forgot. This was basically an over-glorified quickie they were having.

She stroked him just a little harder, paying attention to the sounds he made while his mouth moved on to her collarbone.

Roquette was all kinds of hot and bothered.

He was hot as hell and dangerous, and so far, their sexual chemistry seemed on point.

Things were looking pretty good from her position.

She stroked around the head of his cock, her fingers getting just wet enough with his pre-cum before she began stroking him again.

He definitely seemed to like that.

"F-fuck," he moaned, the word broken and trembling.

"I get the feeling it's been a while for you," Roquette said, wanting to tease him just a little more.

He huffed at her, his mouth finding her breast, kissing the swell before taking one of her nipples between his lips and teeth.

Roquette's spine arched helplessly. She sucked back a hard breath, hardly able to stand the sudden, shocking sizzle that shot down right to her belly.

Smith sounded a little too cocky when he pulled back. "And I get the feeling I'm not the only one."

His hands moved down, down, down, between her legs, stroking her sex. They touched each other, hot and heavy while panting for breath, the clenching in Roquette's belly and the tremors in her legs shoving it in her face that Smith was right.

It had been so long since she'd had anyone other than her own hand and maybe a vibrator.

And the more she used those, the less pleasurable it had started to feel. The more lonely.

This was so much better. It suddenly didn't matter if she was wrong with her crazy certainty that he was her match. It didn't matter if this turned out to be a one-time thing. The only thing that mattered was someone was kissing her and touching her like she was a beautiful treasure, and she wanted to bask in that feeling for as long as possible.

He felt the same. She could tell by the way he moved. In how he kissed her hard, like he was taking what he could while he had the time.

Smith pulled away from her for only a moment, rushing back to the bags by the wall.

"What are you doing?"

"I saw condoms in here."

Her single brain cell hummed and whirred as it tried to process, and then she understood only when he came back to the bed, tearing open the little package.

Right. Fuck. How could she forget?

"Of course. Need protection," she said, grinning like she'd been on the same page the entire time.

Meanwhile, Roquette had been two seconds away from letting him inside her with nothing between them.

That had never happened to her before either. Thank God one of them was being responsible.

Shit, why did it have to be the vampire's bodyguard, though?

But then she didn't care again as her whole existence centered around getting laid once more.

Roquette curled her legs around Smith's waist, pulling him closer as he slid the condom over his hard cock. He was big, and she was desperate to feel him, desperate for *more*, needing him inside her like she'd never needed it before.

Part of her felt embarrassed for being so eager to get laid. At being so horny that she nearly forgot basic sex-ed. Here she was, at the Baer sisters' party, looking for a fated mate and desperate to be fucked by a guy she barely knew but had a *good feeling about*.

And then it was nothing but even better feelings when he pushed inside her.

Her eyes widened, her mouth dropped, but no sounds came out as Smith began to pump in and out of her. Roquette gripped his shoulders tighter, pulling him closer, needing it, needing him.

"Fuck," he moaned against her neck as he thrust in and out of her. That familiar tremble in his shoulders came back as he gasped heavily.

Roquette replied with a moaning sound that was full of pleasure.

"You'll need to be quiet," he said, and Roquette was ridiculously offended.

They'd barely done anything, and he already thought he could make her scream, did he?

She grabbed a fistful of his short hair, yanking his head back so she could glare at him. "You *wish* you could make me scream."

Her words had the desired effect. His green eye flashed, and the red one glowed dangerously.

Smith *was* dangerous.

But then he was kissing her again, his hips kicking forward and back, and oh, that was so nice. That was exactly what she wanted.

She really did try to keep it down. The sounds of their heavy breathing sounded so loud, though. She wasn't exactly screaming his name, but it was difficult to bite back on the moans, groans, and whimpers that left her throat as he fucked her and her body clenched around him.

Everything felt like it was vibrating.

"Wait, wait," she gasped.

He stilled abruptly. "What? What is it?" He sounded a little impatient, which, Roquette supposed, was to be expected in their current situations.

"Does your, uh, penis vibrate?"

He blinked and jerked back. She got the feeling he would have stepped away from her had he not already been inside her. "What? No! What are you talking about?"

"Oh, I thought I felt...." she glanced down between them.

He was still looking at her like she was off her rocker.

She supposed that was only fair, all things considered. "You just make me feel good," she said, grabbing the back of his head, yanking him down, and making him kiss her again.

There, a nice, smooth recovery.

At least she hoped so. Either way, he started moving again, rolling his hips, stretching her open, and touching everywhere inside her that could be reached with his hot, hard...

She moaned against his lips, kissing him now just to

keep herself quiet because he was doing something to her that shouldn't have been possible.

It was wrong. She had to be mistaken. There was no way…

He grabbed her hand, using his human hand, not the mechanical one, and pressed them into the pillow beside her head, lacing their fingers together in a way that made her all melty inside.

He'd already made her see stars.

Her heart swelled, and the feeling inside of her screamed for her to stop denying the truth. *Damn it, Roquette! You're a shifter, and shifters know instantly when they've found their mate! Why are you denying it? Why do you refuse to believe that the thing you've always wanted is finally here?*

"Come," she demanded, clenching her legs around his waist, pushing back against him in an irregular rhythm while her own body almost reached her orgasm.

Smith pressed his face to the side of her throat, kissing and biting. He was going to leave so many hickies on her, but Roquette wanted them all.

That mounting pressure inside her, the sizzling that rushed up and down her legs, making her toes curl as she tried in vain to hold the sensation back, finally got the better of her.

"Kiss me," she rasped, needing it. "Right now."

He delivered, kissing her just in time to swallow down her moan of pleasure. The loud one. The one she wouldn't have been able to keep back without his help as her entire body clenched around him.

He shuddered and groaned into her mouth, his tongue pushing against hers, tasting her. Roquette pushed her fingers back through his hair and gripped tight. There was no way she wasn't hurting him with how tightly she clenched his hair, but he didn't say anything while he rode out his orgasm.

The entire session couldn't have lasted more than a few minutes.

But it felt like a wild ride.

The best of Roquette's life.

"Wow," she said, heart slamming, puffing for breath as she sank back into the comforter and grinned up at Smith. His eyes were closed. He seemed to be in pain.

"Hey," she cupped his cheek. He leaned into it, but that pained look didn't fade. "Are you okay?"

"No. He isn't."

CHAPTER

SIXTEEN

The familiar, cold voice was enough to make all those happy feelings Roquette had inside her fly away. Like a gust of winter wind came in and stole it from her.

Smith cursed, pulling out of her, leaving Roquette feeling cold and vulnerable, naked on the bed while he adjusted his clothes.

He didn't entirely leave her, though. He shielded her with his body while she scrambled for her clothes.

"Aaron, this isn't exactly what I thought you wanted to do with your time when you said you were going to interrogate the party guests," Lilly said, her voice as frosty as ever.

"No, I suppose it wasn't," he said, not turning his back on the woman.

Meanwhile, Roquette realized that her shirt was across the room. By the door.

The door with a broken frame.

How the hell did she manage to bust through the door without either of them—

Oh. Stupid question. They'd both been a little distracted.

Smith seemed to notice her issue, and he took off his overcoat and handed it to her.

Roquette accepted it, unable to look at him. Whatever moment there had been was totally gone, and all she could think about was covering up. At least she had her pants. His coat was more than big enough to cover her boobs, even almost going down a little to her knees.

All she needed was an oversized belt, and it would look like she was trying to make a purposeful fashion statement.

When they were both decent, Smith stood. Roquette followed his lead, though kept behind him, even though a piece of her wasn't entirely sure that he would offer any more protection, other than his overcoat.

But an even bigger piece of her told her to not give up on him. To not allow this whole fucked up situation to poison the fun they'd just had.

And the future she was sure lay before them.

Smith looked at Lilly now, right at her, his shoulders squared, as if he hadn't just been caught having sex with the woman Lilly wanted to question and maybe kill.

"I don't believe she has any connection with the other raccoon," he said stiffly, as though he were a soldier answering his commanding officer.

"They look *exactly* alike," Lilly said, her voice dripping with hate.

Roquette, ever the chatterbox, couldn't help herself. She couldn't just stand around and let people discuss her. She slowly raised her hand. "Hi there, hello."

Lilly looked at her, eyes wide, mouth twisted, as though she couldn't believe Roquette would dare speak to her... or at all.

Roquette continued, ignoring Lilly's look of distaste. "So,

okay, I know that you probably don't like people stealing from you. I wouldn't either, but I swear, I had nothing to do with what happened to you. No connection. None."

"You smell the same too," Lilly sneered.

What?

Smith glared at her even harder than Lilly did, and Roquette could hear the silent demand for her to shut up emanating toward her from both of them.

The strangest part was that, from Smith, it felt more like a warning, and from Lilly, the aura of a threat was all over her.

Right. It was a mistake to talk because this lady clearly didn't want to listen.

"Let me search a little while longer," Smith said. "I won't be distracted again. I just needed to get that out of my system, but now I'm ready to focus. So far, I haven't seen any sign of the other woman. Or your property."

The fuck... Roquette held her tongue this time. *He's just saying what Lilly wants to hear. Don't take it to heart. The sex wasn't that insignificant.*

Though she wasn't sure she could believe it. She was too primed for self-deprecation, and it was easier to believe that he regarded her as worthless than to think he might actually care.

Then she processed the rest of his words.

Wait... did Smith call Dallas *property?*

Did Smith think of himself as Lilly's property, too?

Lilly nodded, seeming to calm down, but just as Roquette was starting to feel like maybe everything would be alright, she pulled a small black device from her pocket, and Smith tensed.

Her perfectly sharp fingernails tapped on the device,

and Smith grunted. "Ma'am," he said, his teeth gritting and his legs locking stiffly.

"What are you doing?" Roquette cried, diving toward Smith, only to be swatted away by Lilly.

The woman had closed the gap between them so quickly that Roquette hadn't seen her move, and she hit Roquette so hard that she sent her flying back into the bed.

"Stay out of my business if you want to keep breathing," Lilly hissed.

Meanwhile, Smith brought his hand to his face—his human hand, since the other seemed locked into place along his side.

Though Roquette could only see from behind Smith, she knew he was touching the side of his face that had the fake, red eye.

The hand touching it trembled. He was in pain. The rising color in his neck and the tightening of his jaw gave it all away.

"Stop!" Roquette cried, bracing for another blow from the vampire.

But Lilly didn't pursue Roquette. She stayed focused on Smith, her finger remaining glued to the device. She gently pushed upward like she was increasing the intensity of whatever it was that was happening to Smith. His body quivered harder—the parts of him that had the autonomy to move, anyway.

"Cut it out!" Roquette pleaded

Roquette moved to leave the couch, having no idea what she would have done if she had reached her target. She didn't have the chance to find out, though. Lilly gave her that look again, the one that was both offended and surprised that the little peasant raccoon girl was getting up in her space, right as Smith reached out with his natural hand and grabbed Roquette, yanking her behind him.

Then he hunched over from the pain of whatever Lilly was doing.

He'd tried to protect Roquette.

Through her distress from watching Smith suffer, a swell of something warm and affectionate rose up within her. Still, that didn't take away from the fact that he looked like he was going to pass out.

"Lilly, please," Smith said through his teeth. His hand came to his eye again, and Roquette could suddenly hear something strange.

A tiny piercing noise, a buzzing similar to the one her ears made from time to time when they were getting ready to pop. This one was like that but multiplied by a hundred.

And that was just what she could pick up. There was no telling what it sounded like to Smith.

And no telling what pain came with it.

It seemed to be mostly focused in his head, while paralyzing his mechanical limbs.

Like she was trapping him in his own body, and Roquette fucking *hated* this woman for that.

"You aren't thinking of straying from me, are you, Aaron?" she crooned in a falsely sweet tone.

"No," he replied through clenched teeth.

Roquette started searching through the pockets of Smith's overcoat. There had to be something there.

Too bad the bitch was so fast. Roquette was a skilled pickpocket, and she could have easily stolen the device from Lilly's hand. A raccoon shifter was no match for a vampire, though.

Wait, even better. Smith's holsters were still on the bed.

Roquette didn't know how to use a gun, but Lilly didn't need to know that.

She reached back, grabbed the holders, and pulled the gun free before pointing it at Lilly.

"Stop what you're doing Right now," Roquette commanded. She had no idea if the safety was on, but if it wasn't, at this range, she was pretty sure she could shoot the vampire in the chest.

Could vampires be taken down by bullets?

Roquette prayed so.

Lilly listened, removing her finger from the device and looking at Roquette as though surprised before her evil smile quickly returned. "And what will you be doing with that?"

"I'll be putting as many holes in you as I can if you don't put the phone down."

"Stop," Smith said, gasping for breath, but with Lilly's finger off the phone screen, he was able to move his legs again.

He stumbled toward Roquette, and she felt like he was trying to shield her with his body.

But who? Was he shielding Roquette from Lilly? Or Lilly from Roquette?

Yeah, no. Roquette took a step away from the bed, moving so she wouldn't be forced to lower her weapon.

"I don't care what you owe her. She doesn't get to do that to you," Roquette said. "And the bitch doesn't get to threaten me either. I didn't do anything to do her."

The more she thought about it, the more enraged she felt.

This wasn't just some over-entitled bitch who was out to get revenge on the person who stole something from her.

This lady used people. She made people like Smith feel

like they owed her, and when they didn't do exactly what she wanted, she punished them. She wanted to torture and hurt the people who had already escaped her, and she wanted to hurt Roquette just for looking like someone else.

That was fucked up, and Roquette wasn't going to lower the gun.

"You think you can shoot me?" Lilly sneered, stepping closer. "Try it, you oversized trash rat."

Roquette stepped back. "Are you fucking crazy? Cut it out!"

Another step. "Are you even holding that correctly?"

Roquette had no idea. And she was pretty sure she'd heard that holding a gun wrong and firing it could take off someone's fingers.

But something told Roquette that Lilly didn't know if she was holding it right either.

In fact, Roquette was pretty sure this bitch never held a gun before any more than Roquette had.

Roquette straightened her back, toughening her stance. "Back the fuck off."

Lilly did not take another step closer. She did smile pleasantly, though, like she was the one still in control of the situation.

Christ, she was hard to read.

Roquette got why people might want to avoid this lady. Why Smith was scared of her.

Scared for himself and Roquette.

"Aaron, take the weapon from her," Lilly commanded.

Oh shit.

Smith straightened and looked at Roquette, his green eye seeming to say, *I'm sorry.*

Oh shit. Oh shit. Oh shit.

"Roquette," he reached out with his human hand while

his mechanical limbs still seemed somewhat sluggish. "Give me the gun."

She didn't want to. Everything inside her told her that this crazy bitch was going to make her disappear. Maybe amputate her limbs and give her body parts that wouldn't work if she mouthed off or tried to save someone.

"Smith," she said, still looking at him because, for some dumb reason, her stupid brain wouldn't let her look back at Lilly, who was supposed to be the real threat in the room.

But she couldn't stop looking at him.

Wanting this to not be real. Wanting to beg him to not do this to her, a virtual stranger he'd fucked quickly on a guest bed three minutes ago.

He reached out, gently taking her hand, forcing her to lower the weapon.

She wanted to keep it raised. Roquette didn't want to let it go, but now that his hand was on her, it was as though everything was done and over with. It was too late. There was no getting out of it and no going back.

Smith exhaled a hard breath when he had the gun in his own hand. He pulled back the top piece, looking into the chamber.

Roquette's heart stopped. She couldn't breathe. She couldn't think. She'd just given up her one chance to get out of there relatively unharmed.

"There's my good boy," Lilly said. "Now, let's—"

The sound of gunfire cut off her words.

CHAPTER

SEVENTEEN

THE SOUND WASN'T EXACTLY LOUD. OR MAYBE ROQUETTE'S BRAIN told her that it wasn't. It was more of a muffled popping noise, but the look on Lilly's face, her red lips dropping open in a shocked *oh*, said that Roquette wasn't the only one who was stunned by this new turn of events.

It took Roquette a second to realize where Lilly had been shot. In the chest. The little hold was there, a touch of steam curling outwards, blood dripping.

The vampire made a futile attempt to touch the device again, but Smith moved quickly, firing another shot. This time at Lilly's hand.

Lilly might have been too shocked to cry out the first time, but the second time she was shot, she raised her bloody hand and screamed loudly and horribly enough that there was no way the party downstairs wouldn't have heard her, no matter how loud the music or chatter.

Her pained scream turned angry as she charged at Smith.

Roquette moved to the side, avoiding the raging vampire and keeping her eyes on her own target.

The little black device was on the floor, wide open and waiting for Roquette to grab it.

The moment she had it in her hands, she touched her finger to it, relieved it wasn't fingerprint locked.

The little rectangle seemed like it could be a small off-brand smartphone or tiny tablet. At least it wasn't complicated to figure out.

Another shot fired off as the two others in the room struggled, and Roquette cringed, rushing into the corner to be as small as she could be.

It was fine, the shot seemed to go to the ceiling as Smith and Lilly fought, but Roquette couldn't pay attention to them.

She immediately looked at the options in the app Lilly had been using to hurt Smith.

The fact that there was fucking app for….whatever this was, probably should have shocked her, but of course, it didn't.

She knew she was in the right spot when it showed her Smith's picture. His full name, his age, including all the modifications he had.

Her heart would have hurt for him if she'd had time to process everything. For now, Roquette tapped everywhere she could, searching for whatever it was she needed that would allow Smith to be free of Lilly.

"You! Give that back!"

Roquette looked up just in time to see Lilly making a mad dash to get to her. The woman's hair was wild around her shoulders, no longer perfectly done up, and her eyes were murderous.

Smith stopped her from reaching Roquette by wrapping his arms around her from behind and holding her back before she could do anything.

Not for lack of trying, as her legs kicked up, expensive heels flying and hitting the wall on either side of Roquette's head.

Fucking hell.

Roquette got back to work, searching through the app.

There was a notification to restart and delete all files. That seemed like something that would take away her control over Smith's body.

But would it take away Smith's control of his own parts, too?

Shit. She didn't know what to do.

Then the commotion in the room quadrupled as new people rushed inside. "What the hell is—"

Roquette wasn't looking up at them, still too busy figuring out what she was supposed to do to help Smith.

"*Lilly?*"

Roquette did look up for *that.*

A man stood there. Maybe a little taller than Smith. He wore a red sweater, probably in keeping with the holiday theme of the party, and right next to him was...

A woman who looked *way* too much like Roquette. Well, like Roquette but with dark hair instead of blond.

"Holy shit."

The two women said it at the same time.

Others in the room seemed to think Lilly needed help, as they rushed to her.

"Don't touch her!" Smith shouted, barely holding onto the woman who reached back to claw at his face with those disgustingly long nails.

The man in the red sweater joined the fray, helping Smith.

"Dallas!" Roquette's doppelgänger—Rita—screamed.

"Wait!" Roquette shouted.

She shouldn't have bothered. Everything was chaos, no one was listening to anyone else, but it was clear that Dallas was there to help Smith.

Because he was the guy who had been stolen from Lilly.

The other person who was like Smith.

Of course he wouldn't want to help the vampire bitch he was trying to escape from.

There were many people in the room now, and Lilly was struggling harder than ever against the two cyborg men, but they seemed to have the upper hand.

"What do you have there?" Rita asked, seeming to have caught sight of the device and become interested enough in it to cease trying to stop Dallas from fighting Lilly.

"I..."

"I'm Rita," she said.

"I figured. I've heard a lot about you tonight. Or at least, heard that I look like you and that you've stolen something from that vampire bitch."

"She thought you were me?" Rita asked, her face pinched in worry.

"No, I think she knew we were different but thought I must be related to you or something and in on the heist or whatever." Roquette shook her head. "Sorry, not important right now. Here's what's up. My name is Roquette, and I've grabbed this device that Lilly dropped. It seems like she was using it to... hurt Smith."

She'd been about to say control, but that didn't seem entirely right. Smith had control, and he was using it now.

"Oh my God," Rita gasped, looking over Roquette's shoulder at the device.

" "Right? Is your boyfriend—Dallas?—in here too, or did you already take him out of it?"

Rita shook her head, looking through all the data that

scrolled by the screen. "No, he wasn't... he hadn't been hooked up to an *app* yet."

She sounded like someone who'd just recently adjusted to a new world of madness, who was now learning about another whole new level of insanity.

Which, it kind of was.

"I think you should delete it," Rita said, sounding more confident about it than Roquette did.

Especially considering the man Rita cared about wouldn't be affected by it, but Smith would be.

"I'm worried if I do anything that will affect the app, that Smith might lose control of his cybernetics. That he might not be able to walk or see."

Or do so many other things that she probably wasn't thinking about at that moment.

Rita pressed her hand to Roquette's shoulder. "Dallas can move around just fine without an app. Delete it."

"It's probably backed up to a cloud or something..."

"Give me that," Rita swiped it and began poking around.

Roquette felt panicked. She was holding Smith—and a load of other cyborgs—in the palm of her hand.

"She's dumb as fuck," Rita laughed. "Assuming she wanted this option in here. Otherwise, maybe whoever designed this wanted there to be the chance for the cyborgs to be released, because right here, in the backdoor settings, look. Freedom mode."

"Freedom mode?" Roquette repeated, remembering the words she'd shared with Smith earlier about that very topic.

Rita began going through each cyborg in the app and setting them to freedom mode. "Look," she pointed. "Once it's on, you can't disengage it. This is *final!*" she laughed in glee and kept going.

Roquette wanted to scream at her to just go to Smith's first, but she also dreaded what might happen.

When Rita did get to Smith in the app, the world seemed to slow down.

Roquette looked across the room. Lilly screamed and snapped her teeth at Dallas while Smith barely held onto her, keeping her back.

"Here goes nothing," Rita said, tapping the confirmation on the device.

Smith's knees buckled, and he fell backward.

CHAPTER

EIGHTEEN

Smith fell, and something in Roquette snapped to attention at the sight.

She couldn't leave him there. Couldn't let him lie on the floor while the other big guy, Dallas, did all the heavy lifting.

Especially when it looked like everyone else in the room and outside it was too busy watching the train wreck to even bother with helping.

Some people were even pulling out their phones and actually recording.

Roquette hated them the most, but they were in the very back of her mind as she ran to Smith, grabbing him under his arms and pulling him away as Lilly managed to break her hold off from Dallas just enough to lunge.

Just for Rita to step in and punch her right in the face.

Lilly hardly appeared phased, at least not physically. However, she did stop in her tracks, once again giving that look that said how she couldn't believe any of this was happening.

"You struck me."

Rita pointed a finger at her, looking like a badass. "You stay the hell back, or there'll be more of that."

Roquette wasn't so sure how good of a threat that was supposed to be when Lilly didn't so much as have a scratch on her.

Except for where Smith had shot her, of course. There was definitely blood from all of that.

But that was all. There wasn't much of anything else to suggest her fight with Dallas and Smith had left that much of an impact.

"Let go," Smith said.

"What?" Roquette had practically dragged him to the other side of the room. She would have liked to take him out of the room entirely, but there were too many people blocking the way. Too many people looking for a show.

To her shock, Smith managed to lift one of his knees, putting his foot firmly on the carpet. He groaned, pushing himself away from Roquette, trying to stand.

Her relief at his movement was so great that she let him do it all on his own.

Which is what he wanted. She could see it. He didn't want to lean on her as he pushed himself to stand.

She was right there, though. Hovering when she probably shouldn't be.

She couldn't help herself.

She couldn't clear the painful lump in her throat, either.

She'd thought she had destroyed his chances for walking, but as he stood, even if a little shakily, it was clear he wasn't just getting lucky.

He was *standing*.

Which meant he was also still *seeing* out of his mechanical eye.

He brought his fake hand up, fingers clenching and unclenching beneath the glove he wore.

While he stood, Roquette fought against the trembling in her knees, the urge to sink down.

He was all right. He was going to be okay. Roquette and Rita hadn't destroyed him.

Lilly, on the other hand, looked murderous.

"You too, Aaron? Another cyborg smitten for a *trash rat?*"

Roquette hated how Lilly called him Aaron. Like she was trying to get personal with him or make fun of him.

Which didn't make sense since it was his name, but it was just something in her *voice*. In the way she crooned it.

Smith glared at her. "I quit."

Lilly pressed her lips together. She didn't say anything, but Roquette could taste the change in the air.

Especially when Lilly looked at her.

Smith re-joined Dallas, and the two men with cybernetic upgrades could barely hold the outraged vampire back.

Roquette got the feeling Lilly really, *really* wanted to come after her and cut her throat open.

Well, at least she has a reason now, and not just because I look like Rita.

Dallas and Smith were so focused on preventing Lilly from lunging forward at Roquette that they were unprepared for her to take a side leap away from them and jump straight through the glass window.

Dallas surged forward, a final attempt to take her out, but he didn't make it. He missed her entirely as she flew outside with a crash.

The people standing around screamed. Smith and

Dallas moved to the window, looking out and seeing nothing.

"We won't find her," Smith said, sounding tired.

He and Dallas looked at each other.

Roquette was pretty sure they hadn't officially met, but the way they stared at each other, like they knew each other, or knew they had something in common, was enough to dial down the intensity in the room.

Rita looked down at Roquette, frowning. "So, about this lookalike thing... do we know each other?"

Roquette shook her head, but Harmony took that moment to finally appear, pushing her lithe frame through the throng of people. "Of course you know each other. You're family!"

Rita frowned at Harmony. Roquette did, too.

Then they looked at each other.

Taking in the similarities. It wasn't looking into a mirror, but, yeah, Roquette definitely understood why Lilly looked at her and thought there was a connection.

Harmony turned to her guests, waving them all off as though they were being burdensome. "All right, enough of this. Enough. Back to the food and drinks. I'm not paying for all of this just so a broken window can ruin our party."

She managed to shoo most people away. Some lingered, but what a Baer sister wanted, she got.

Smith cleared his throat. "I think I need to have some words with that woman."

Dallas nodded, still eyeing Smith like he wasn't so sure about him. "Yeah, we can all use some... level headed advice on what the hell is going on."

No shit was what Roquette wanted to say, but she was too caught up in what just happened.

Harmony calling Rita her family. Harmony acting like this was normal.

Like there was anything about this that was on the level.

"I think Roquette needs to get dressed first," Smith said.

Roquette shook her head, holding his overcoat a little tighter around her. "I'm keeping this."

He looked at her funny, his brows furrowing before the corner of his mouth quirked. Just a little. "You're keeping my coat?"

"Yeah. Of course I am." She marched past him, grabbing her big cozy sweater, glad no one had taken it. "Did you forget I'm a thieving raccoon?"

And as far as she was concerned, the coat that smelled like him was her reward for putting up with Harmony's weird games.

Rita glanced around suddenly. "Wait, did you two have sex in this room?"

NINETEEN

ROQUETTE, SMITH, DALLAS, AND RITA FOUND THE BAER SISTERS in another room of the giant mansion.

Roquette wouldn't have been shocked to find out that some people had decided to leave the party, but from the sounds they heard downstairs, most people were drunk enough to want to stay and keep enjoying the music, food, and company.

Right. Weird happenings and a little danger were normal for this sort of thing. Roquette did come here half expecting this sort of thing, after all.

She just didn't expect the sisters to smile at her, at all of them, the way they did when they met up with her after such a big commotion.

The blond one—Sheri—smiled, holding out her hand. "Lilly's device, if you'd please," she said before anyone could speak a word.

Roquette, wearing a few more clothes beneath the overcoat she stole from Smith, handed it over.

Sheri looked at it, tapped around, and then smiled. "You did well."

Roquette wished she wouldn't be so mysterious.

"So, what was all that about?" Roquette asked.

Dallas and Rita were holding hands while Roquette stood next to Smith. As if they were both still strangers.

Roquette tried not to stare at them, especially at Rita.

Harmony gestured to Rita and Dallas. "If you wouldn't mind filling your long-lost relative in, please."

Rita cleared her throat, glancing up at Dallas. "Right, well, uh, when I first met Dallas, he wasn't as plugged into Lilly's system as...." she gestured toward them.

"Aaron," Smith said.

"Right, as Aaron was. We didn't have to worry about an app making all his extras go haywire, but we figured there was still the chance she could track him."

Roquette understood immediately. "You lured her here to get her phone?"

Dallas made a seesawing motion with his hand. "Not exactly. We knew she was probably watching us, but we didn't know when she'd make a move. We've kind of been living a life of looking over our shoulder, just waiting." He glanced over at the sisters, who were pretending to be preoccupied with other things in the room, such as the whole slew of alcohol options on a shelf.

Rita continued. "Anyway, we didn't think you or anyone else would get involved. The party was supposed to be safe enough, too many people, but I guess it was just bound to happen this way."

"It is when Harmony gets involved," Sheri interjected.

"What can I say, I knew it would be the best time to get the girls together." Harmony shrugged, a smug smile on her face.

Roquette snuck a glance at Esme, still wondering if she had anything to do with Roquette and Aaron meeting. The woman's face was blank, and Roquette started to doubt that she'd actually had any involvement at all.

"We just thought we'd be the ones to make the first move," Dallas continued, looking pointedly at Smith. "You fine with leaving her behind?"

"If I'm off her database, then yes," he said.

Roquette noted the way he clenched and unclenched his mechanical hand. As though confirming to himself that it still worked.

Roquette's mind raced. "Wait, so you were waiting on her to make a move... but now what? You just continue waiting? Now *we* have to wait too? She's going to show up again at some random place with a new cyborg bodyguard?"

Rita, Dallas, and Smith all exchanged looks, though none verbally confirmed her suspicions.

They didn't have to.

She had wanted to come to the party to find... someone. *Her* someone. She'd thought that was Smith, thought maybe this Lilly stuff had something to do with her.

Instead, she stumbled into someone else's drama, and now she felt stupid.

Deep breath. It was okay.

Roquette was going to be an adult about this.

It wasn't all bad. She had herself a little adventure, got laid with one handsome devil, and helped the good guys win. It was actually a good thing.

"I don't mean *we* like, together we," Roquette babbled. "I mean, me on my own. Him on his own. You two together, though..."

Smith looked at her, his expression hard to read, and she was pretty sure it had nothing to do with his mechanical eye.

"So, you both aren't...?" Rita asked. She looked at them, then back at Esme, who chose something in what looked to be an expensive bottle.

"I think we should let them figure that out, Rita." Esme finally spoke. "Who wants a drink?"

Roquette didn't want a drink. She wanted to get the hell out of there. Facing Lilly again one-on-one sounded more desirable than staying in that room full of thick humiliation.

"Sweetheart," Sheri said. "You look like you need some fresh air. Aaron, why don't you take her downstairs. Get her a non-alcoholic drink and some snacks? It's been a long night."

"Sure," Smith said, shocking Roquette since she didn't think he'd be open to doing anything for anyone for a while.

"And come back when you're freshened up." Harmony waved. "You still need to have your family reunion."

When they were outside, the door closed behind them, and the wide-open hall letting her breathe a little better, Smith spoke. "Do you know what she's talking about? The family reunion thing?"

"She says I'm related to Rita."

"Maybe you are. You both look alike. Cousins, maybe?"

Roquette shrugged. "Possible, I guess. I don't know my entire extended family."

She braced herself against the wall. Her hands shook. Coming out here wasn't helping so much because she still had to deal with Smith.

"Should I call you Aaron?"

He tilted his head a little. "That is my name."

"I've been calling you Smith, like Agent Smith." She faced him, struggling to hold his gaze.

"You can call me Smith." He smiled softly. "I like that you call me something different from everyone else."

"Even Lilly?"

His mouth thinned. "Lilly is like an abusive mother. There's always a threat in there."

"And what do I talk like?"

He came to stand next to her. "Like someone who *really* didn't get that she was in danger."

Roquette grinned a little, feeling slightly better.

"I think it turned you on, though." She nudged him. "Getting to protect this little idiot damsel."

"You're not an idiot, and you're definitely no damsel," he said, looking her right in the eyes. "I can't believe you pointed my gun at her for a guy you barely know. Also, I'm going to have to teach you how to hold a weapon."

"You... will?"

He nodded, crossing his arms. "I appreciated the bravery, but I was more scared that you would blow off your thumbs."

Roquette shivered, holding her hands together. She liked her thumbs right where they were.

"So, you want to teach me."

"No partner of mine is going to hold a gun the way you did."

She froze. "Partner?"

"I'm not calling you my girlfriend. It's too... juvenile. I'm too old for that word. Lover, if you want."

Now her heart was pounding.

Smooth. She was going to be calm and sophisticated about this.

"Okay."

He looked at her. "Okay?"

He was asking her so much more. She could sense it in his tone.

Asking if they were really going to be a thing. If she didn't mind sticking it out with him. If she didn't mind all his... extras. She heard all of that in that single word.

"Yeah. Okay," she said, taking his hand. "We should go back inside, have that talk. I'm sure you and Dallas will have stuff to talk about, too."

He smiled at her, gripping her hand tight, their fingers lacing together.

Roquette was on cloud nine as they opened the door back to the sisters, Rita, and Dallas.

And because she was a little shit who couldn't help herself, she had to add, "My boyfriend and I are ready to chat!"

The End.

...actually, we're just getting warmed up!

Roquette, Smith, Rita, and Dallas are back in each of the following stories in this series... you see, there are more relatives for them to reunite with, and they have a lot more to do before they finally face off with Lilly in Book 5: Etched in Brass!

ABOUT THE AUTHOR

USA Today Bestselling Author Mandy Rosko is a videogame playing, book loving chick. She loves writing paranormal romances that range from light steamy to erotic, and has some contemporary and historical romances as well. You can find her on all sorts of platforms, including Twitch, where she does writing sprints, crafting, and video gaming!

Get all the latest news from Mandy by signing up for her newsletter: subscribepage.com/mandyroskobooks

As a bonus for signing up, you'll get her starter library, including Burns Like Fire, Sold to the Enemy, and The Vampire's Curse!

facebook.com/MandyRoskoRomance

instagram.com/mandyroskodraws

amazon.com/Mandy-Rosko/e/B008ETBVFW

bookbub.com/authors/mandy-rosko

goodreads.com/mandyrosko

youtube.com/UCD1z6r06dKoN-0WdUbi1pAQ

ALSO BY MANDY ROSKO

PARANORMAL ROMANCE

Blood Secrets

Darkness Awakened

Passion Awakened

Beauty Awakened (Coming Soon)

Eve Langlais' FUCN'A

I'll Be Dammed

Trash Queen

Chillin' Out

Bits and Bobs

Poisoned Kisses

Goddesses of Vengeance

Angel's Fury

Shape Up or Shift Out

A Rose by Any Other Name

Winter of Discontent

Sea of Trouble

The Better Part of Valor

Etched in Brass (Coming Soon)

Shifter Hospital

Alpha Medicine

Second Chance Alpha (Coming Soon)

The Aquaterrestrial Task Force

Get Kraken

Shark Bait

The Nightshade Guild

Mage to Disobey

Magic Confined

Defying Time

~

Crimson Moon Hideaway

(Amazon and KU Only)

Double Booked with Her Ex

Flame and Mist

~

Learn more at mandyrosko.com

SHAPE UP OR SHIFT OUT SERIES

A Rose by Any Other Name
Winter of Discontent
Sea of Trouble
The Better Part of Valor
Etched in Brass